THE ANGRY MAN

D1527510

G·K
Hall
&Co.

Also by T. T. Flynn
in Large Print:

Death Marks Time in Trampas
Long Journey to Deep Canon
Night of the Comanche Moon
Rawhide

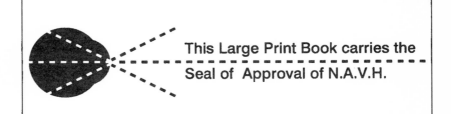

This Large Print Book carries the
Seal of Approval of N.A.V.H.

THE ANGRY MAN

T. T. FLYNN

G.K. Hall & Co. • Thorndike, Maine

Published in 1999 by arrangement with Golden West Literary Agency.

G.K. Hall Large Print Paperback Series.

The text of this Large Print edition is unabridged.
Other aspects of the book may vary from the original edition.

Set in 16 pt. Plantin by Rick Gundberg.

Printed in the United States on permanent paper.

Library of Congress Cataloging in Publication Data

Flynn, T. T.
  The angry man / by T. T. Flynn.
    p. cm.
  ISBN 0-7838-8523-7 (lg. print : sc : alk. paper)
  1. Large type books. I. Title.
  [PS3556.L93A82 1999]
  813′.54—dc21   98-54329

THE ANGRY MAN

ONE

There had been sixteen savage days of it, and nights too — riding, fighting, watching, waiting for the next attack. On the Texas Plains, Comanches had looted Tom Cantrell's trail herd. West of the Pecos, Apaches had stolen most of what was left.

Four of the crew had been killed. Earlier, Jess Macey had been murdered in the Texas settlements. Now, smoke signals were lifting from the foothills to the south when Tom Cantrell rode forward to George Sell, at the point of the herd. and ordered, "Keep them bunched close ahead of the wagon."

George Sell, a quiet man with sweeping brown mustaches, a fierce man in a fight, said briefly, "Think we'll last through another ambush?"

Tom Cantrell, a long, muscular young man, scoured and leaned-out, smiled with a total lack of mirth as he turned on the sweaty saddle and eyed what was left. Two hundred and twenty-six gaunt steers and cows were hoarsely bawling as they scuffed dust westward toward Fort Ross and the Frio Plazas. They had been twelve hundred. Most of the *remuda* was gone. "We'll get through!" Tom said slowly.

"Still think all this was planned against you?"

"Everything that's happened," Tom said, "points that way. If I could guess what Jess Macey tried to tell us —"

"Jess," George Sell said, "tried to tell something."

They walked their horses side by side, both thinking of that far-off, dark alley in a little Texas settlement, where Jess Macey had sprawled inertly and muttered. *"Hand! His ha-n-n — !"*

Jess had been gathering legal documents from scattered ranches. Only the signed documents had been taken from him. No money. George Sell said tersely, "You guessed then we'd have trouble. We sure had it!" George reined over to check the long-striding lead steers.

Tom dropped back, trying to judge where the attack today would come. Two miles to the south the first low foothills lifted, piling, climbing to the great forested peaks which were the ramparts of the eastern Apaches.

In the west, ahead, bold ridges ran down along the skyline to a stark pinnacle of rock. It would happen, Tom guessed, somewhere this side of that soaring pinnacle. He had no idea that a girl was standing by the pinnacle, gazing hopefully toward his herd. He would not have cared. Nerves and watchfulness tightened as the slow herd advanced . . . And it was Eagan, on the flank ahead, who suddenly stabbed an arm south and wheeled his horse back.

Riders, barely visible, were emerging from the first foothills. Swiftly Tom used his binoculars. His arm went up in reassurance as Eagan's running horse swung around to a walk beside him.

"White men!" Tom said. He gave the binoculars to Eagan, and added, "About thirty miles to the Frio Plazas. We'll make it now."

For the first time in days, Tom relaxed. This morning the little mirror on the wagon side by the water keg had reflected sandy hair hacked off with a knife, and his dark face gaunt and smoldering. His eyes had been bloodshot. They felt gritty under the lids and tired; he was tired all over, to the bone.

"They got that roan Box 6 gelding with a white stocking on the right front leg!" Eagan exclaimed. "Remember that'n?"

"Comanches got that roan," Tom said as he took the glasses. He looked through the binoculars, and the gaunt planes of his face hardened. "Since Jess Macey was killed, I've been looking for white men who might be trading with the Indians. Eagan, don't speak of the roan when they get here."

Eagan shrugged and rode out with Tom to meet the strangers: six men, well mounted, heavily armed, blanket rolls tied behind their saddles, grub sacks and canteens dangling. And out of Apache territory, with a horse which

9

Comanches had stolen on the Plains!

The white-ankled roan was reined alongside Tom's horse. It had the familiar Box 6 brand on the right flank. Now there was no doubt.

The rider's greeting was genial: "I'm Matthew Fallon. This a Texas herd?"

"What's left of a Texas herd," Tom said. "I'm Thomas Cantrell."

Fallon sat the stolen roan gelding in jaunty confidence, right hand thrust carelessly in the coat pocket of his gray suit. His brown straw sombrero had a swagger of silver braid around the crown. He looked cocky, prosperous, prideful as he inquired, "Had trouble?"

"Too much trouble," Tom said. "I've lost men. Lost most of the herd. Smoke signals in the south this morning suggest more trouble today." Tom paused, and then suggested, "With you men helping, we'll do all right now."

"We're riding north in a hurry," Fallon said without interest.

"I had twelve hundred head," Tom said. "Nine men in the crew. You see what's left. Old Sam Butterworth, driving the wagon, has a bullet-crippled leg. We're low on ammunition. We need help."

Fallon said indifferently, "We can't help guard every strange herd which expects trouble. But I'll always trade for a profit. I'll buy your herd here for cash."

"How much?"

"Two dollars a head. Keep your wagon. You

can reach Fort Ross or the Frio Plazas by tonight and be safe."

Eagan gave a jeering whistle. Fallon swung sharply in the saddle as if suspecting a signal. The startled roan snorted, jumped. Fallon blurted an oath as he went off balance. His right hand jerked out of the coat pocket, and Tom's stare narrowed and hardened.

The hand was twisted and claw-like! From the dark alley far back in Texas, Jess Macey's mutter came again, *"His hand! . . . Ha-n-n — !" . . . Here was a hand,* on this stolen roan horse! Puzzling bits of murder and disaster fell into place with this. Eagan's lobster-red face was startled too as Fallon almost viciously shoved the twisted hand back into the coat pocket.

"Ride to the wagon," Tom quickly ordered Eagan. "Tell Sam Butterworth we'll get no help from these men." Eagan's red face was showing belligerence. "Now!" Tom ordered sharply.

Reluctantly, Eagan rode toward the wagon. Fallon glowered after him. "That man's known the Army."

"How far away is that wagon?" Tom asked.

Fallon's genial manner had vanished. The crippled hand, Tom guessed, was a chink in the man's cocky pride. He listened to Fallon's surly guess about the wagon, "Maybe a hundred and fifty yards away. Why?"

Eagan had reached the wagon. "Sam Butterworth," Tom said evenly, "is a tough old hickory knot. Sam went into Mexico in '46 with

General Wool's men. He used to trap beaver with Kit Carson. Sam can drop buffalo all day at better than a thousand yards with his Sharps rifle and rest sticks. At a hundred and fifty yards, Sam won't miss a man who leaves him with a bad leg for the Apaches."

"That," Fallon said, "sounds like a threat."

"It's advice," Tom said coldly. "Get off that roan horse that was stolen when the Comanches hit us!"

At the great rock pinnacle miles to the west, the girl Tom Cantrell had never seen was making a hopeful guess to her companion. "Judge, it could be the Cantrell herd."

"Or, *ipso facto,* any other herd," was the Judge's calm reply.

He was a tall old man in white shirtsleeves, red suspenders, and a high, shabby stovepipe hat, tilted slightly on his sweeping gray hair. The rock pinnacle towered over them. The Judge had strolled back from the stunted cottonwood where Virginia Bratton stood, and their two horses lazed with reins dragging. The tall stovepipe hat gave extraordinary length to the Judge's shirtsleeved figure as he drew slowly on a black cheroot and squinted intently into the west along their backtrail.

Virginia Bratton was peering eastward where the green foothills reached into haze-hung distance. Far out there on the vast sweep of landscape, a tiny white object lay motionless upon the distant, shimmering land. When one looked long and intently, the white dot slowly sank into hidden folds of the earth and vanished. Finally, gradually, it reappeared, canvas on a moving wagon. The barely visible black dots by it were cattle. Virginia said, "They'll not get this far today."

"Probably not," the Judge agreed.

"If we ride to meet them, we can't get back to the Plazas until after dark." Virginia was rueful. "All this ride, without knowing whether it is the Cantrell herd."

The Judge faced around. "Three Apaches," he said calmly, "rode out from behind that first ridge, cut our tracks, and went to cover in an arroyo out there. They're watching us."

One lived with this sort of thing and made the best of it. "You advised me not to ride so far, and I kept going," Virginia said contritely.

The Judge said cheerfully, "Suppose we follow an old fogy's hunch and ride on and see if it is the Cantrell herd."

"So it's that bad?"

"*Expertus metuit,*" the Judge said wryly, "which is to say, 'Having had experience, he fears.'"

The first fear touched Virginia. He was an old man, tall, benign, oddly and awkwardly and impressively dignified when he wished. And always he was shrewd, with depths of droll wisdom forever surprising her. The Judge's squint now at her long linen riding skirt and

13

flat-brimmed straw hat told exactly nothing, really. She remembered that the Judge was a feared poker-player.

The Judge gave her a hand up to the side-saddle, mounted his own horse, and pulled the tall hat firmly onto his forehead. Long gray hair curled down against the back of his neck. He might be seventy. Virginia herself did not know. His shrewd, lined face had carried this pinkish, youthful glow back through her memory. Now the Judge said cheerfully, "Go slowly until we're down the slope out of sight." His small smile considered her. "Then ride, Ginny, like the Old Snake was close."

Virginia adjusted her skirts and surveyed him dubiously. "It will be a hard ride for you."

Wrinkle by wrinkle his smile spread. "If we're followed, watch how young an old mossback can get." His squint tightened. "More of them may be infesting the landscape. No matter what happens, keep going until you reach that herd. *Keep going,* Ginny!"

Virginia tightened the chin cords of her straw hat. "I'm ready," she said.

At the trail herd, Matthew Fallon was flaring at Tom Cantrell, "This roan stolen from you?"

"I've a bill of sale, all marks on him written down," Tom said coldly.

Temper, chagrin darkened Fallon's heavy features. "My horse broke down! I bought this roan

14

from an Indian! If I have to pay again, I will! How much?"

Eagan was returning from the wagon at a swinging canter. On the jolting wagon seat, behind the long six-horse team, old Sam Butterworth's long, heavy Sharps buffalo gun lay across his lap. Sam was watching them. "You knew the Box 6 brand meant the roan had been stolen from some white man," Tom said curtly.

"How much for the horse, Cantrell?"

"We buried men after that raid on the herd, Fallon. Get off!"

Eagan reined alongside as Tom watched Fallon's broad face go dull, muddy with malice. "Cantrell, you're being a fool!"

Softly, coldly, Tom said, "You offered two dollars a head. Is a two-dollar horse worth it?"

Their horses were walking. The hot sun struck between them on the long grass and baked earth. The question hung between them for tightening seconds. "No! Not worth it!" Fallon finally blurted under his breath.

"Then get off!"

Fallon's head came around. His eyes had a dark shine. "You're the starry-eyed lieutenant who turned in his commission at Fort Union to try to start a big ranch, aren't you? You went partners with a land speculator named Rogers, who had land scrip he'd picked up cheap. You two used the land scrip and some cash to get title to most of the good water north of Fort Ross." Fallon yanked the roan to a halt. The claw of a

15

right hand stayed concealed in the gray coat pocket as he dismounted. "Fools," Fallon said in a strangled voice, "usually get what they deserve!" He called to his men who had pulled up, "One of you put my saddle on your horse!"

Eagan dropped his rope around the surrendered roan's neck, and kept silent until Matthew Fallon and his riders were heading on north through the thin dust drift behind the herd. One man rode awkwardly straddled behind another. The extra saddle was balanced in front of a second rider. Eagan's boiled-looking face was redder when he finally asked, explosively, "Did y' see his hand, Lieut'n't? Remember what Jess Macey said, back in Texas before he died? *A hand!* It didn't make much sense!"

"It makes sense now," Tom said.

"You let him ride away!"

"His crippled hand didn't prove anything." They were walking their horses toward the wagon, which had started on. Tom was sober and thoughtful. "It all fits, Eagan. We were watched from the time we reached the Texas settlements and started talking to ranchers who'd lost stock in Indian raids."

"Reckon Fallon an' his bunch were in the settlements then?"

"No proof," Tom said. "But Fallon is here in New Mexico now. We'll meet him again. I took the roan from him to see if he'd talk while he was angry, and try him in a showdown."

16

Eagan's wide red face grinned. "You wet down his fire."

"He used his head, Eagan. He's dangerous. Never get careless about that man."

"You can handle him, Lieut'n't," Eagan said comfortably.

"Stop calling me 'Lieutenant'. We're out of the Army now," Tom said.

Eagan had been a sergeant, the pride of barracks and stables, and a sulphurous memory on officers' row. Tom Cantrell had been his line lieutenant. Now Eagan was indulgent: "I'm lookin' after you, Lieut'n't, until we're back in." Eagan virtuously believed it.

Eagan had never been cursed, Tom thought wryly, with the beckoning dreams which had driven into new, unsettled country — and sometimes destroyed — the younger men of the Cantrell generations. Eagan took the roan horse toward their scanty *remuda* and Tom rode to the jolting wagon.

Sam Butterworth called, "That was a cold-blooded bunch, not helpin' us!" A small, irascible splinter of a man with a wisp of iron-gray chin beard, wearing a disreputable leather shirt belted at the middle with rope, Sam hunched on the hard wagon seat with his feverish left leg at an awkward angle.

"Remember that man Fallon," Tom told Sam. "He'll be waiting for us."

"Better shoot him first," Sam advised.

Tom grinned at the dour little man on the

17

jolting wagon seat. Sam met trouble without scruples. "I might have to kill him," Tom said, and the hard, deep anger returned as he rode up alongside the herd. His partner, Steve Rogers, was waiting expectantly at the ranch. Cattle and horses were gone now. Men were dead. He and Steve had used most of their money.

Steve Rogers had trusted Tom Cantrell. Rebuilding what had been lost was a driving, personal thing now. And if Matthew Fallon was the man who had planned all this disaster, what lay ahead would be doubly dangerous. Tom rode thinking about it and watching the foothills closely. And when he finally sighted movement, the swiftly focused binoculars brought the green scrub cedars and spiky *amole* clumps on the nearest hill crest leaping close . . . *An Apache!*

One Apache, sitting a dun horse, moccasined feet toed-in under the horse's belly. Red cloth circled the Apache's forehead. A red cloth streamer dangled from one brown arm. The gun held carelessly in one hand appeared to be an efficient Spencer repeating carbine.

On that distant hill the Apache had a greasy look as he spat and scratched his bare ribs. A moccasined heel kicked the dun horse lunging, sliding down the steep ridge slope, and Tom lowered the binoculars. His arm wave started Eagan back to the wagon. Tom rode there too.

"Get under the canvas, Sam, ready to shoot when the wagon stops!" Tom ordered. "Eagan will drive."

Sam halted the long six-horse team and grimaced as he swung his injured leg back over the board seat. Eagan stepped up on the wagon, and stood for a moment in front of the seat, watching the lone Apache, down off the ridge now, heading toward the herd at a leisurely trot.

"Just lookin' at him rises my gooseflesh," Eagan said. He looked into the west before he sat down. "Lieut'n't!" Eagan blurted suddenly. "Gimme them glasses! *Quick!*"

Eagan peered through the glasses a long moment. "A white girl an' a old gent!" Eagan's cluck was approving. "She's a young one. Pretty! They're headin' toward us on the whip! Three Apaches chasin' 'em!"

"You idiot!" Tom said, and tersely he ordered, "Sam, get inside! Eagan, drive out from the cattle and stop when Sam tells you to!" Tom slashed with the rein ends and rode ahead. His beckoning arm brought the three other men of the crew to him.

"Hold the cattle here," Tom said. "George, come with me."

"What's shapin' behind them hills where that Apach' showed?" George Sell asked.

"We'll know!" Tom said, and took George Sell in a furious ride out ahead into the west. The pale drift of dust out there was clearly visible in the shimmering distance. The girl took shape on a sidesaddle, riding beside the man. The quirt on her wrist, Tom decided, could have lashed her horse into the lead, and she was holding back.

19

George Sell bent for the carbine in the scabbard under his leg. Tom did the same. The three Apaches were whipping furiously trying to close. The girl's horse and the man's horse were ridden-out. Flaring nostrils and froth-spattered withers grew clear as the flung dust of their run swept close. Tom waved them on, and as the drumming rush went by, the girl's wan smile brushed his glance.

Her companion held a long stovepipe hat in one hand. Gray hair streamed back. He rode bent forward, bobbing awkwardly. Yet, from some reserves of spirit behind the face gray with exhaustion, the old man brought the long hat toward his forehead in salute as he swept by.

TWO

Miles to the northeast, distant now from Tom Cantrell's herd, Matthew Fallon rode apart from his men in silent rage. He knew the five men were covertly, derisively thinking of the surrendered roan gelding. When he finally swerved his horse over to them, Fallon was cocky and a little arrogant, as usual. "Anyone see any sign of the boy around Cantrell's outfit?" he called.

Joe Sloan, a hardfaced, surly man, straddled awkwardly behind Red Kane and visibly resenting it, called back, "Whyn't you ask Cantrell while he was takin' your horse?"

Fallon stared coldly. "Why didn't I ask Cantrell about several things, Joe?"

"Dunno."

The slow lope eased to a trot, then a walk, as the other men listened with interest. "I'll tell you why," Fallon said with sudden vicious malice. "That old goat on the wagon, Joe, could have cut you in two with his big buffalo Sharps. He would have at a word. What do you say to that?"

Joe Sloan licked his lips. "Ain't sayin'. Just bouncin' on this horse's hard back."

The other men stared curiously, sensing obscure meaning in the clash of words. Fallon eyed them all disdainfully. "Most of you are alive now because I think for you. Cantrell and his men were ready to fight. Where's the profit in a gun battle over a worthless horse, which belonged to Cantrell anyway? The Apaches will handle Cantrell and his outfit!"

Fallon pulled his horse to a stop and dismounted, keeping his right hand in the coat pocket. The other men stepped down, stretching, relaxing while their horses started to nip grass. There was no derision now.

"Joe, saddle another horse," Fallon said curtly. "You're riding to the Frio Plazas. If Cantrell gets there, I want to know what he does next."

"Want him shot?" Joe Sloan asked, matter-of-factly.

"Cantrell is too much man for you," Fallon said coldly. "He'd shoot you, and know I'd sent you, and be on his guard. I'll take care of Cantrell."

Red Kane said, "Why bother about Cantrell?"

"He's starting the first big ranch in this part of the Territory," Fallon said. "Others will follow. Men like you will be run out." He watched them thinking about Cantrell narrowly now, and said, "Where's young Lee Bratton?"

Red Kane grinned. "After you left for Texas, Lee Bratton beat a hoss-buster at your Gallinas ranch all bloody. 'Bustin' 'em too rough!' Lee said; 'A hoss is better'n a man most times!' he yelled, an' hit him."

"Lee Bratton is a wild young stallion himself," Fallon said with faint contempt. "His hotheaded ideas will get him shot. Where did he go?"

"Took most of his pay in a blood bay stallion that was the pick of the bunch they were breakin'." Red Kane said with amusement. "Said he was headin' for Las Vegas."

"Find Lee Bratton, Red," Fallon said, after a moment's thought. "Tell him some new horses are coming in from the trading camp over on the Tongue. There's a big yellow-gold horse with a white mane and tail that I picked for myself. I've never seen a finer one. Tell Lee he can have the horse, and his pay too, if he'll hustle back."

"For a hoss like that, he'd go anywhere," Red said. "Likely he's racin' hosses an' swappin' hosses around Vegas or Santa Fe. I'll bring him back."

"Where will you be, Fallon," Joe Sloan asked, "if there's word about Cantrell?"

"Finding out how things have gone while I was in Texas," Fallon said. "Look for me at Largo Canyon or the Gallinas ranch." He added, "Cantrell may not get past those Apaches today."

The hope stayed with Fallon when he rode on. Cantrell's men would be outnumbered today. They were short of ammunition. Any hour now, the last of Cantrell's outfit, and Cantrell too, might be wiped out.

Virginia Bratton had noted the old Judge's youthfully gallant salute when they passed the two riders. The worst of her tight fear had eased off. She had been afraid the Judge would not last. He was too old for this kind of desperate riding.

Their horses were blowing dangerously and weakening. Virginia slowed the wild run and wondered if one of the two strangers were Thomas Cantrell. Perhaps the younger man, clean-shaven, dark, angry-looking as he had waved them by — She hoped with lifting spirits that he was Cantrell. All she had heard, all she expected made the prospect pleasant.

The Judge called, "That was close, Ginny!" It had a weary sound; but under his white shirt and red suspenders, the Judge's lean old shoulders were visibly bracing with new energy. They both looked back as a gun slammed dully; then another. An Apache pony plunged sideways in a swirl of dust, its rider sprawling off and bouncing up.

"That should stop them," Virginia called to the Judge. Her interest reached ahead to the bunched, restless herd held by two riders. "Not enough cattle to be the Cantrell herd," she told the Judge.

"Any herd is good enough now," he answered dryly.

Virginia had watched the canvas-topped wagon in the far, shimmering distance. Now powder smoke bloomed lightly from the side of the wagon. Over near the foothills, a lone, breechclouted rider leaped off his falling horse and ran back toward the hills. Other riders poured down the ridge front . . . seven . . . thirteen, Virginia counted. She thought they were coming on, but the running Indian swung up behind a man. They all rode back up on the ridge and vanished.

"It doesn't look good," Virginia said.

The Judge nodded. The wagon driver's wide red face held an understanding grin as they pulled up by him, and Virginia slipped from the sidesaddle. Her knees were weak. Her horse drooped, its lathered sides heaving. The Judge dismounted from his equally exhausted horse and said, "Young man, a pleasure to be with you."

"I bet."

Virginia pulled off her straw hat. Her hair was damp at the roots. She felt disheveled, shaky as she inquired, "What herd is this?"

"Cantrell's herd, ma'am. He's comin' now."

The rider nearing the wagon was the younger man who had waved her on. The officers at Fort Ross had served with him at Fort Union. Their fond tales had made him sound rather fabulous — tall, laughing Tom Cantrell, joyful with a bottle or with ladies, cards or soldiering, to the surprising day he'd turned in his lieutenant's commission and left to start a new ranch in the wildest part of New Mexico Territory. The stories she had heard at the fort did not fit this lean man who swung off his blowing horse and called, "Sam, what d'you think?"

The answer came through the weathered wagon canvas, "They've counted us, Tom. They'll ambush us an' stampede the hosses an' cattle."

"There's enough of them to try for the wagon too," Cantrell said.

The Judge had set his tall shabby hat back on his disarranged gray hair, and was shaking out the black coat, which had been tied behind his saddle. "Thomas Cantrell?" he inquired.

Cantrell had pulled off his black hat and was wiping a blue kerchief over his gaunt face. "Yes," he said.

"This is Miss Virginia Bratton," the Judge said. "I'm Barnaby Polk, her lawyer, and guardian also in some matters."

Brown, indifferent eyes flicked over Virginia. "Miss Bratton —" Cantrell said without interest. He was blunter to the Judge, "You almost lost this young lady."

"I was to blame," Virginia said. "I kept riding, hoping we'd sight your herd." She smiled faintly, anticipating his surprise. "I'm your new partner."

"My partner is Steve Rogers," Cantrell said.

The Judge explained, "Steven Rogers, your former partner, is dead."

Cantrell seemed to freeze. An edged hardness entered his demand: "What happened?"

"Rogers," said the Judge, regretfully, "was

shot off his horse between the Frio Plazas and the ranch. No one seems to know what happened. Mrs. Rogers sold her inherited half of the ranch partnership to Miss Bratton, and returned to Maryland."

A look of tired, smoldering anger crossed Cantrell's gaunt face. "Steve too!" he said, and then, flatly, "I can't use a new partner."

Nettled, Virginia said, "You have a partner, nevertheless." She turned to her drooping horse.

"Steve and I agreed that if either of us died, the other would buy his share," Cantrell replied. "You don't fit my plans, Miss Bratton."

Virginia turned back to him, holding her straw hat by its leather ties. "I have plans of my own, Mr. Cantrell."

"*My* plans, ma'am, are all I'm interested in."

Her black hair, caught back and pinned, barely reached his broad shoulders. She had to look up at his weather-scoured face. "We own a ranch together, Mr. Cantrell. Judge Polk will tell you so."

"All this can be discussed later," the Judge suggested.

"Where is the mixed herd of over a thousand head, which Mrs. Rogers said was being purchased in Texas?" Virginia persisted.

Cantrell's sober look considered her. "Two hundred and twenty-six left. Indians got the rest. I'll buy you out, Miss Bratton. Haven't the cash now, but my note will be good."

"I don't care to sell."

"I've had men killed in Texas," he said, patiently. "The partner I counted heavily on is dead. There will be more trouble connected with this ranch. Bad trouble. A helpless girl simply won't do for a partner."

"I'm not helpless!"

For an instant she thought Cantrell's disturbed look was flecked with humor as he considered her. Then his hard somberness returned as the man inside the wagon called, "Tom! That Apache who rode out first is Senya, the kid says!"

"So that's him?" Cantrell said with interest. "He led the bunch that ambushed us four days ago."

"They had luck fust time; can't blame 'em for tryin' again," the voice said.

"This time we know they're around," Cantrell said. He turned to the Judge. "Your horse is run-out. Get on the wagon seat with your carbine. The lady can ride inside."

"I'll ride my horse," Virginia said coolly. She turned to catch up the dragging reins, and unbelievably Cantrell's arms caught her up from behind. Outrage broke from her. "Put me down!"

Silently Cantrell carried her to the rear of the wagon. His closeness reeked of horses, tobacco, powder smoke, sweat. The arch of his deep chest was against her. She was breathless and helpless as he deposited her in hostile silence, like a sack, on bedrolls inside the wagon. "You've made

28

enough trouble today," he said curtly, and was gone.

It was hot under the wagon canvas, and a sour voice chuckled, "Welcome, partner. I'm Sam Butterworth, an' I oughta have better sense, too, than be here."

He sat on a bedroll near the middle of the wagon, a lean little man in a greasy leather shirt. His scant gray chin beard looked awry and bristling. A heavy Sharps rifle was propped on crossed, brass-bound rest-sticks in front of him, its muzzle in a hole he had cut in the canvas. Virginia dropped her hat and stumbled to her hands and knees as the wagon started with a jerk and a rising screech of dry axles. She could see the Judge's lanky figure on the wagon seat beside the driver. And as she balanced unsteadily on the bedrolls, a thin, chocolate-brown figure sat up beyond Sam Butterworth.

"Who is *that?*" cried Virginia. At first sight, in the hot shadows, the figure looked Apache! Wild hair hung Indian style below the ears and was hacked off across the forehead. The tails of an oversize gray shirt, belted with a piece of rope, hung almost to small, bony knees. Then Virginia saw that the wild hair was brown, and the blue eyes of a white boy stared impassively at her.

Sam Butterworth said, laconically, "Says his name is Eddy Morton. Comanches got him an' his mother in Texas, an' traded 'em to the 'Paches. Cantrell almost shot him when the kid snuck up to the wagon las' night."

"And the mother?" Virginia asked quickly, concerned.

"Says he run away to get help for her. That buck I put afoot was Senya, who had the kid for a son. If he guesses the kid is here, he'll get him."

Virginia looked at the small, sun-browned figure in the baggy shirt. "Eddy, how old are you?"

The boy gave her an impassive look, old beyond his possible years. Slowly, as if his tongue and mouth were stiff with the language, he said, "Eleven," and looked away, ignoring her.

The six-horse team was trotting. The heavy wagon swayed and groaned. Canvas slapped on the wooden bows as Virginia made her way forward unsteadily over the bedrolls and picked up one of three carbines beside Sam Butterworth. "We buried the men who owned 'em," Sam said simply.

Silently he handed her a sheath knife. Virginia slashed an opening in the canvas and looked out. Apache, Comanche, Navajo and Ute had been in the background of her life. The three toy-like riders she could see over near the foothills were an accustomed part of this wild, lonely land. "Will the others ambush us?" she wondered aloud.

Sam Butterworth's shriveled face showed no visible concern. "Can't tell what an Apach'll do." He scratched a hip, and grumbled, "The kid musta brung lice!"

The lurching wagon came to a halt ahead of the bunched herd. Virginia looked out the back and saw a rider hazing the few *remuda* horses off to one side. Cantrell and two other men were moving the cattle slowly toward the first hills. They fired handguns. The cattle lumbered into a run. The three riders swerved out of the dust and turned back toward the wagon.

"The son-of-a-gun!" Sam Butterworth muttered. "Givin' 'em away!"

"Part of them are mine," Virginia said.

"I'd tell my lawyer." Sam Butterworth scratched again, and looked reproachfully at the boy.

Cantrell rode to the back of the wagon. Virginia called indignantly to him, "Half of those cattle are mine, Mr. Cantrell!"

His gaunt face regarded her without expression. "Get them if you like." He spoke past her to Sam Butterworth. "There's an arroyo ahead, Sam, which comes out of the hills. I think the rest of the rascals are in it, waiting for us. More, probably, than we've seen. A coyote ran out of the draw and looked back. I'm hoping the cattle will bait them away."

"They'd rather have the horses, Tom."

"We'll need the horses," Cantrell said. "Those three Apaches over by the hills are trying to hold our attention. If the others are in the arroyo ahead, I'll pull them into the open."

"They'll stay hid 'til the last minute, Tom."

31

"The arroyo swings northwest," Cantrell said. "We'll go closer to it, then turn north, as if we're missing it. There's no other cover close. If they want us, they'll have to come out in the open."

"They'll come, if they've got a chance," Sam Butterworth guessed. "An' they'll fade back if they don't win quick."

"Keep the lady safe," Cantrell said, and reined away.

The groaning roll and lurch of the wagon continued on. The *remuda* was brought in close. Sam Butterworth gnawed a chew of tobacco from a dark twist and relaxed on the bedrolls. It was hot under the canvas. Virginia's mouth was dry as she thought bleakly of Cantrell, *What a man for a partner!*

Abruptly the wagon turned north. Sam sat up and adjusted the long, heavy rifle on its rest sticks. "If they come, don't git rattled," he advised Virginia.

She smiled wanly. Her hands felt hot, moist as she thrust the carbine barrel through the opening in the canvas and looked out. The drop-off into the arroyo was visible not two hundred yards to the west. Only grass, low cactus, and clumps of rabbit weed lay between. Cantrell, his riders and the *remuda* were on the east side of the wagon.

"I've never shot a man," Virginia said aloud.

"Sight an' shoot," Sam Butterworth said calmly. "Easy."

Virginia tightened as Cantrell's great-lunged shout lifted outside the wagon, "Pull up!"

Horses carrying painted, breech-clouted riders with high moccasins were bursting up over the arroyo bank. Scattered out, they raced toward the wagon, and began to shoot. Sam Butterworth's big rifle bellowed. A rider toppled off his horse.

The Judge had left the wagon seat. Cantrell and his men had dismounted. The driver fired his carbine. The sights of Virginia's carbine wavered as she lined them on a naked chest painted in black and red, and squeezed the trigger; then quickly closed her eyes.

The dismounted men were shooting. Sam Butterworth's long rifle spoke again. Other Apache horses were swerving, running without riders. All of it was unreal, Virginia thought as she aimed again, fired, and again closed her eyes. When she looked a moment later, the attack was dissolving in dust and floundering flesh, and the surviving Apaches were galloping back toward the arroyo. Cantrell shouted, "Let's go!"

The six-horse team surged into a run so quickly the Judge barely regained the seat. Virginia had fired twice and probably had not hit anything. Sam Butterworth pointed to three bullet holes which had not been in the canvas.

"They shoot high," he said casually. The Apaches had vanished into the arroyo, leaving riderless horses and bodies in the open. Presently Sam Butterworth scratched again, cast another reproachful look at the silent boy, and lay back on the bedrolls, closing his eyes. "That," he said, "baked their potatoes!"

THREE

Traveling fast without the slow herd, the wagon crossed the big arroyo without incident. Tom Cantrell, riding watchful sweeps out ahead, pondered somberly the high, hopeful plans he and Steve Rogers had made. . . . The new herd was gone, and most of the *remuda*. Jess Macey had been murdered in Texas. Steve Rogers had been murdered near the ranch. Half the crew was lost. Money had run out.

And back of it all loomed the man named Matthew Fallon. In the dangerous weeks ahead, there would be more of Fallon, Tom decided. He made plans as the long miles ran into a blazing sunset, and the massive Black Butte marked where the little valley of the Frio turned through the foothills to Fort Ross.

Eagan drove the wagon pitching, sliding down the sandy Frio bank. The jaded horses gulped at the shallow Frio current as Tom rode splashing to the wagon. Virginia Bratton was sitting between the old lawyer and Eagan. She regarded Tom with hostility.

"Sam Butterworth will go to the post surgeon

in the wagon," Tom said. "You two can ride your horses to the Frio Plazas with the crew."

Virginia Bratton said coldly, "Will you be at the Upper Plaza tomorrow to discuss business?"

"If I can buy you out with a note, ma'am, I'll make a point of being there."

"I'll not sell!"

"The herd's gone; there's no other business to discuss," Tom said indifferently.

Her flush was visible. "We own a ranch together, Mr. Cantrell. I'm a full half-partner in everything. Judge Polk will tell you my rights."

The old lawyer said calmly, "As administrator of this young lady's inheritance, and that of her younger brother, Lee Bratton, I advised the purchase of this half-interest in the ranch. It's all legal."

"Is a brother in this too?" Tom demanded sharply.

"Miss Bratton used her own money." Barnaby Polk leaned out from the wagon seat and offered a worn leather cigar case.

Tom bent from the saddle and took one of the villainous black cheroots. He guessed this tall old man knew every trick in the law books and a few more. And they'd be used for the Bratton girl's benefit. "I'll be at the Upper Plaza in the morning," Tom said, and put his horse up the opposite bank.

Eagan drove the wagon lurching up to level ground. The girl and old man mounted their horses. Virginia Bratton reined over to Tom. "Mr. Cantrell, what about the boy?"

"He's going to the fort with me."

"He needs a home. I'd like to take him."

Tom regarded her with faint malice. "He left a good home, Miss Bratton. An excellent Apache wickiup, where he was the adopted son of a sub-chief named Senya, petted, learning their ways, and rather liking them."

"No civilized boy could like living with blood-thirsty savages!"

"He was taken from a two-room soddy in Texas," Tom said calmly. "He'd had to help with the hard work and got his lickings; too many lickings, I gather. He's had more fun with the Apaches."

"He ran away."

"To get help for his mother, who is not the petted son of a sub-chief," Tom said deliberately. He called to the wagon, "Want to go with this lady, son?"

"No," came back through the canvas.

Tom put the cheroot between his lips and watched Virginia Bratton bite her red lower lip and wheel her horse away. Eagan stayed with the wagon. Gray twilight condensed about them as the wagon wheels crunched on the narrow rough road up the Frio valley to Fort Ross. Night came blackly, and Eagan pulled up as a sentry's challenge cut the night ahead. Tom called out. The sentry shouted, "Corpr'l t' guard! Post number seven!"

"Flugelmeir!" Eagan yelled. "What's E troop doin' at this coyote post?"

"C an' E troops come from Fort Union six weeks ago."

Tom called, "Who's commanding?"

"Major Alcorn."

Eagan's "Ah-h-h!" held covert, amused meaning.

A man's past, Tom reflected ruefully, was never surely behind him. Eagan knew that Isabel Alcorn was probably here at Fort Ross with her father.

A summons for the doctor went through the post gate ahead of them. Eagan halted the wagon beside the dark parade ground, in front of long, low adobe barracks; and Tom said, "I'll see Major Alcorn if he's available."

He rode across the dark parade. He heard brisk steps on a porch at the end of officers' row, hurrying toward the wagon; the doctor, no doubt. Then a dimly-seen white dress moved off the adjoining porch into the starlight.

"Tom Cantrell?"

"Isabel?" Tom rode to meet her and swung down.

"Tom! How nice! I was visiting the Dourte's and heard them calling the doctor." Memory filled in the details of Isabel's oval features, blurred in the starlight. She was taller than most girls, amusing, with the assurance of the commanding officer's daughter. "We're the tag-end of the regiment now," Isabel said. "Ordered here to Fort Ross and forgotten. Tom, how did it go in Texas?"

"Lost half my men; most of the *remuda* and all the herd."

"Tom! I'm sorry!" Then quickly, Isabel said, "You can come back into the regiment."

"Who has some clothes to fit an eleven-year-old boy?" Tom asked, evading her suggestion. He explained about the boy.

"I'll see to everything," Isabel said.

Minutes later, waiting alone in Major Alcorn's small parlor, Tom smiled wryly. Isabel liked to manage. She had decided, evidently, to manage Tom Cantrell back into the regiment.

The peace of the major's shabby little parlor was soothing as Tom stood by the front window, hat in hand. The long days and nights in the saddle, the savage fighting, bone-weariness and endless hammer of ill fortune, faded a little inside these whitewashed adobe walls. The few pieces of battered furniture were proof that Major Alcorn, as usual, was not trying to fare better than his junior officers.

Alcorn's energetic voice was audible from a back room, directing the orderly: "These to the adjutant. Tell him that mail for Fort Union must be ready by breakfast call in the morning."

The orderly hurried out through the narrow center hall. Major Alcorn entered the parlor with a half-smoked cigar in his hand. His shock of dark blond hair and his neat blond mustache were still only lightly touched with gray. Restless energy radiated from the lean figure.

"You look like short rations and hard riding, Tom. Cigars in that box on the table. Sit down and tell me about it." A shabby rocker creaked under Alcorn's solid weight. Even relaxed, with his blue blouse comfortably open at the neck, he showed alert vigor.

Tom selected a cigar and dropped into another creaking rocker, smiling faintly as he recalled the rawhidings Alcorn had given him. Every one deserved.

Alcorn was the General's trouble-man, which probably explained this new command at Fort Ross. The enlisted men in the barracks and stables called him Indian Charley, because of his grinding patrols or bloody skirmishes. Alcorn harried raiding Indians fiercely. He could be a help in what lay ahead, Tom hoped as he said, "I can't brag, Major. I lost my Texas herd and five good men. One man was murdered in the settlements. Comanches hit us hard —"

Alcorn paid keen attention, munching absently on the frayed end of his cigar. "Too bad," he said at the finish. "Going back after another herd?"

"No money left, sir."

"You have a new partner," Alcorn said. "She has visited the fort."

"I met Miss Bratton today," Tom said, without enthusiasm. "Have you any information, Major, about Steve Rogers' death? Who killed him and why?"

40

"A patrol from the garrison we relieved found him, Tom. That's all that seems to be known."

"The boy we picked up," Tom said, "ran away to get help for his mother. He has a boy's faith that she'll get help."

Major Alcorn's face clouded. "I've been thinking about the woman. Not enough men in the garrison to go into the mountains after her in force, which would be necessary. The Apaches would kill her, or move her fast, if we did go in. She's another tragic case, Tom. Too many of them these days. The Indian Agent at Santa Fe will return the boy to Texas. He'll get over it."

"What boy gets over his mother? I'll keep him at the ranch; something may happen."

"Don't give the boy false hope," Alcorn said soberly. "Many women and children have been carried off in the same way. Few return."

"Texas knows it," Tom said. "The Comanche raids were never worse. Homes are looted and burned, settlers killed, captives taken, livestock by the thousands run off."

"It will be stopped before long."

"It's not being stopped," Tom said. "Herds of cattle and horses are run north by the Comanches and Kiowas, and sold for trinkets to traders, who bring the livestock into New Mexico Territory and sell it cheap." Memory of what he had lost himself put roughness into Tom's promise, "I'll stop some of that!"

"That's quite a statement."

"New Mexico holds well over a hundred thou-

41

sand head of stolen Texas stock," Tom said. "I collected powers of attorney in Texas which cover scores of brands that have been raided. I'll stock my new ranch that way, Major."

"Been tried, Tom. Any stock you replevin will vanish before the law can do anything."

"I'll take stolen stock where I find it!"

Outside in the night, the hour call floated from sentry to sentry, and Alcorn sat motionless. His gaze had narrowed. "That means guns, Tom."

"Guns took my herd," Tom said. "Guns killed my men, and murdered Steve Rogers. There's no civilian law in this part of the Territory. I'll make my own law."

Major Alcorn got to his feet and moved to the front window. On his feet also, Tom waited. "You'll be shot if you try it," Alcorn said over his shoulder. "Come back into the regiment, Tom, where you can do some good."

"Not what I want, sir."

"What do you want?" Alcorn inquired, patiently.

"I wanted new land to tame, and build on, Major. That's why I turned in my commission. Now I want back all I've lost, and more!" The roughness came back, smoldering: "It's personal now! I'll break every man I find in the dirty Indian trade! I'll take their stolen cattle and run them out of my part of the Territory!"

"Fort Ross," Alcorn said calmly, gazing out the window, "will tame this part of the Territory. You have five men left, you say, and no money to hire more. Try such a reckless scheme, and you'll quickly be hunted down and shot."

"The Army could help me, Major. Settlers in Texas who have lost their stock deserve help."

"The Army is not meddling in civilian affairs."

"Then I'll manage, Major. Men are coming from Texas to help recover stolen stock. They'll work with me, from my ranch."

Alcorn swung around. "How many men are coming from Texas? When are they coming?"

"I don't know how many men, or exactly when they'll get here. But they're coming. We'll take stolen cattle where we find them."

"Not in my district," Alcorn said. They stared at each other. Alcorn's lean features were tightening. "This part of the Territory is just opening up," he said in an even tone. "The Apaches, and even Comanches from the Plains, are making enough trouble. My orders are to pacify and protect."

"Protect whom, Major? Cattle thieves and buyers of stolen cattle?"

"Texas gunmen taking cattle unlawfully will infuriate settlers and Indians," Alcorn said slowly. "A hornets' nest will be opened. If it happens, I'll intervene."

"And meddle in civilian matters after all," Tom said, holding his temper. "You'll decide, perhaps, who dies, Major?"

"If you'll have it that way," Alcorn said after a moment.

"I'll have it that way!"

43

"You've been warned, Tom."

And it would be this way, Tom knew regretfully as he left Major Alcorn's quarters. The Army, too, would be against him. He paused beside his horse in the starlight, thinking about the violence which undoubtedly lay ahead.

His thoughts turned to the girl who was his new partner. She had mentioned her own plans. She would have the advice of that tall, shrewd old lawyer. And she had a brother. The talk with her tomorrow would bring another clash, Tom suspected as he rode to find Sam Butterworth and the doctor. He had little relish for meeting the girl.

FOUR

The Judge had brought a hickory-smoked Missouri ham from Santa Fe. Virginia was cooking thick ham slices for breakfast when grease popped out of the large iron skillet. *"Ouch!"* Virginia exclaimed. She stepped back from the hot kitchen stove, in which chunks of aromatic cedar wood crackled cheerfully. "It should be his eye!" Virginia said darkly, rubbing her wrist.

The Judge, relishing his morning coffee at the pine table behind her, inquired with interest, "Whose eye?"

"That Cantrell man's eye." Enveloped in a nainsook apron, Virginia stood fork in hand resentfully thinking of Tom Cantrell.

The Judge had slept on a cot in the little parlor of this three-room adobe Virginia had rented on the outskirts of the Upper Frio Plaza. A shaft of golden sunlight through the small kitchen window turned the Judge's red suspenders into gay bands across his lean shoulders, brightened the long gray hair falling down the back of his neck, highlighted the amusement on his shrewd, wrinkled face. "Still want to spit and skewer the young man?"

"Why did he have to be like this?" Virginia said resentfully. "Refusing to have a partner! Losing the herd! And now most of my money is gone!"

"Cantrell has no money left either," the Judge reminded her.

"He's a man!"

"With an angry young lady partner; heaven help him," said the Judge, blandly.

"This is serious," said Virginia. She turned the smoking ham slices with jabs of the long fork. "I hoped a ranch might help Lee settle down. And all I have now is empty land and an impossible partner!"

"So Lee," said the Judge, "is back of all this?"

"Lee and his fine horses and wild ways!" said Virginia unhappily. "He rides all over the Territory to race his precious horses. He fights and gambles. He's friendly with outlaws. And he's getting wilder."

"I hear reports," said the Judge dryly.

"If you'd given Lee his inheritance when he was twenty-one, he might have settled down."

"Tosh!" The Judge was almost testy. "When did easy money cool off a young hothead?" The Judge put down his coffee cup. "I watched you two grow up in Santa Fe, Lee only a year younger. But who protected Lee? Who covered up Lee's mischief? Who told everyone that Lee was the finest brother a girl ever had?"

"He was." Virginia said in a smaller voice. "He is. But Lee needs responsibility. I wrote him to

46

come and help me. And now what is there to help? I can't even have Lee around this man Cantrell. They'd fight. I know they would. All I've done is waste my inheritance."

"Not necessarily," said the Judge. "Cantrell and his partner got title to parcels of land which control all the good water for forty miles north of Fort Ross. The water controls all the free range in that area. Fort Ross will increasingly control the Apaches and Comanches. The foundations of a great ranch are there, Ginny. And you have clear title to half of it."

"And no cattle and no money!"

"Cattle live and die," said the Judge. "The water, the land is important. I control Lee's inheritance for three more years. With Lee's consent, secured legally, I might let you borrow some of Lee's money to buy cattle —"

"Would you?" Hope brought Virginia around — and the fast pound of a running horse held her listening. Whooping exuberance split the morning sunlight outside. "It's Lee!" Virginia ran to the front door.

The plank door burst open as she reached it. Lee bolted in, whooping, "Not a steer or cow left!" His strong arms swept Virginia into a whirling turn. "Heard it in the plaza as I came through!" Lee jeered. "The old man wouldn't hand me fifty dollars of my own money, but he pushed you into a sour cattle deal!"

As Lee released her, she warned, "The Judge is in the kitchen."

Half a head taller, lean-hipped and supple in his denim pants and canvas jacket, Lee shoved his hat back on his rumpled black hair and said, "Now I can beg again for a little of my own money!"

"Lee! Please —"

"He knows how I feel!" Lee stepped to the low kitchen doorway and leaned a hard shoulder against the jamb. "How much crawling does it take this time?" Lee asked defiantly.

"Had breakfast?" the Judge said mildly.

Virginia remembered the ham and hurried past Lee to turn the slices before they burned. When she faced around, Lee was sulkily taking the chair opposite the Judge. "How much do I get today?" Lee demanded.

"In three more years," said the Judge, unruffled, "you'll have all your inheritance. By then, I hope, you'll realize that owning the best horses in the Territory, and playing bad poker, aren't the most important things in life."

"I've owned horses that were better than most men I know," Lee said hotly. "What's wrong with a horse?"

"Nothing," said the Judge. "I like a fine horse myself. As a horse." The Judge drank from his coffee cup and set it down slowly. "But I admire a responsible man more."

Virginia held her breath as Lee flushed angrily. Increasingly, Lee's temper flared easily. Her thoughts went to Cantrell, angry and forceful, and now such a big part of their lives. What would happen if Lee and Cantrell clashed? "Breakfast," Virginia said unhappily, "is ready."

The sutler's building at Fort Ross was a long, low adobe, with the post barbershop at one end. This morning Tom Cantrell was the first customer. Clipped, shaved, scented, Tom stepped next into the sutler's cluttered store to buy supplies for the ranch.

Clean clothes felt luxurious. Breakfast this morning — he was a guest of the bachelor officers' mess — had been a merry meal. While Tom made purchases, a Ute scout watched stolidly, and across the store an enlisted man's wife shushed a fretful baby in her arms. And when the gusto of Eagan's voice lifted in the barbershop, Tom stepped to the doorway and paused, smiling.

Eagan and a half-dozen tough troopers surrounded young Eddy Morton in the barber's chair. Only the boy's thin, small face, dark as an Apache's, and his long, ragged, brown hair were visible above the barber's white cloth.

Eagan was telling the barber, "E troop helped scrub him with scourin' soap last night. We doused lamp oil in his hair to run the bugs out. Then he wanted bear grease to rub on hisself! 'Not even bacon grease on E troop,' we told 'im, and rolled him in a blanket by tattoo, smellin' like the major's clean Sunday shirt."

"Eagan," Tom said through the doorway,

"bring him into the store here when you're through."

"Yes'r."

And when Eagan brought the boy into the store, Tom saw that Isabel Alcorn had managed well, as usual. Shoes and long black cotton stockings, baggy knee-length knickers, and a white shirt were the patched, outgrown Sunday best of some officer's boy. "You look great," Tom said, smiling. He sniffed. "Smell good, too. Now we'll buy you some new duds for the ranch."

Blue eyes in the thin, dark face stared anxiously up at him. The boy drew a breath, "Are they —" He swallowed. "Will the soldiers —"

Tom said casually, "I told the major about your mother. But these things take time."

He watched the thin face turn worried and desperate; and a little later as he walked to the quadrangle he was still trying to put the boy out of his mind. The yeasty fragrance of new bread drifted from the post bakehouse. Outside the guardhouse a glum prisoner was trudging an endless circle with a log on his shoulder. And on the quadrangle, Tom smiled when he sighted Isabel Alcorn emerging from the adjutant's building ahead.

Isabel opened a pink sunshade and waited for him. She looked fresh and summery in a white cambric suit as they fell into a slow walk together. "Father is disturbed about you," Isabel said.

"I gathered as much last night," Tom said dryly.

The old black field hat in his hand had a darker pattern on the front, where the crossed-swords insignia had once shielded the felt from sun and weather. Isabel's finger indicated the darker pattern. "Still in your hat, Tom." Isabel's glance searched his face, "And still in you, too, isn't it?"

"Only the memories," Tom said. His oblique glance was mischievous, "Many memories —"

Isabel colored. "You could come back into the regiment, Tom."

"With all the future ahead? All the excitement and great things to do?"

Isabel regarded his bantering with smiling exasperation. "Still starry-eyed, Tom, aren't you?"

"Yesterday," Tom remembered, "a man named Matthew Fallon called me exactly that — starry-eyed."

Isabel flushed. "Matthew Fallon?"

"Yes."

Isabel bit her lip, then admitted, "Mr. Fallon heard me say it, I suppose. Your name had been mentioned; I said what I thought about your leaving the regiment."

"Who is this Fallon?"

"He has a ranch on the Gallinas, I believe," Isabel said. "He visited Fort Union, and has been here too. Mr. Fallon seems a gentleman. Everyone likes him."

"Evidently."

Isabel's color heightened as she thrust back, "Isn't a pretty black-haired ranch partner most of the exciting future ahead?"

Tom's grin turned annoyed at the thought. "A stubborn, interfering female partner underfoot is the last thing I want!"

Isabel regarded him with smiling interest. "I believe you mean it."

"I do!" Tom said. "And I'll have to get along, Isabel. Promised to meet the young lady and her lawyer in the Upper Plaza this morning."

"Will you be back today?"

"Can't say." Tom lifted his black hat casually as he left her.

Too casually, Isabel decided as she watched him head across the wide, sun-drenched parade with long, easy strides. Tom Cantrell had come back from Texas a changed man. The dark planes of his face had a hard, remote look in repose. *Only his plans matter now,* Isabel sensed, and her conviction crystallized: *Tom is a dangerous man now! Even to a woman!*

Yesterday Isabel Alcorn would sensibly have rejected such a man. Now her pulses beat faster as she stood motionless, looking after Tom Cantrell. Her breathing was shallower as she walked slowly on, absently revolving the pink sunshade.

Tom rode from the fort alone, leaving Eagan to follow with the loaded wagon and the boy. The rough road skirted the singing current of

52

Frio Creek out of the foothills and turned west at the Black Butte. Northward, the empty country reached out to far, smoky horizons, and the Frio ran west through a widening valley to the two Frio Plazas.

The Lower Frio Plaza had been settled first by native families from the distant Rio Grande country. The Upper Plaza was the larger settlement, where stagecoaches and wagon trains came, and the mails and trade.

Steve Rogers had thought the Upper Plaza a friendly place; and Steve had been murdered in the lonely miles between the town and ranch. Any stranger in the Upper Plaza could be the man who had killed Steve; and could be waiting now to kill Tom Cantrell. The wary thought went with Tom past the outlying corrals and weathered sheds to the big sun-flooded plaza.

Low, flat-roofed adobe structures filled the east and south sides of the plaza. The west side held a feed corral and wagon yard. The open, sloping bank of Frio Creek formed the north side of the plaza, and a patrol returning to the fort had dismounted there.

In the center of the plaza, teamsters were hitching long spans of mules to loaded freight wagons. Men, women and children of the town were out in the open, watching the activity. Tom rode toward the dusty, unshaved troopers, watering horses and pack mules down the Frio bank. A dust-floured lieutenant standing on the Frio bank showed fatigue in every sagging line.

Tom pulled up behind the lieutenant's weary back and said, "Fitz, your cot was mighty comfortable last night."

Second Lieutenant Horace Horatio Fitzpatrick wheeled around, bloodshot eyes squinting. "Blast us! The new cattle king!" Smiling, Fitz came to the stirrup and thrust up a hand. "We're out eighteen days!" Fitz said. "South; then west into the Jornado! Hot and dry!" Fitz squinted up. "How about an easy job on your new ranch?"

Tom sighted George Sell ducking under a hitchrack on the south side of the plaza. He lifted the reins and grinned down at Fitz. "Your job's waiting, Fitz. Never hot, never dry, sleep all you want —"

"Look for me!" Fitz called after him.

Smiling wryly, Tom skirted the freight wagons. Fitz, he knew, would never do it. Like Major Alcorn, like Isabel, Fitz would follow the guidon to the end. Tom met George Sell and stepped down from the horse, asking, "How is it?"

George had on his clean denim pants and wore a new gray shirt under his open vest. His hair and brown mustaches were freshly trimmed. George resembled a sober deacon with a gun on his hip. Faint disapproval tinged his report: "Buck Ellis an' Pete Yancey celebrated last night. They're over at the feed corral holdin' their heads."

"They've earned a headache," Tom said tolerantly; then, regretfully, "I left Sam Butterworth

54

at the fort. He may lose the leg."

"It'll finish Sam," George said. "Shy a leg, Sam'll give up. Any help from the Army in what's ahead?"

"Worse," Tom said. "Troops will intervene if Texans help us take stolen Texas cattle."

"So?" George was thoughtful as he rolled a smoke. "That finish your plans?"

"No."

George twisted the brown paper at one end. "Five of us left. Every man in a hundred miles who owns Comanch'-stole cattle, or who's stole cattle, will be at us first move we make."

"Want to pull out?"

George considered deliberately. Mule teams at the nearby freight wagons were trampling dust. Trace chains were jingling, teamsters cursing loudly as George struck a match on the heavy buckle of his gun belt and lighted the cigarette. "I'll stay," George said. "One of the hardcases who was with that Comanch'-trader Fallon rode in last night."

"Which man?"

"The one who give Fallon his horse yesterday. Name's Joe Sloan. He was in the saloon last night. Handy with a gun, I hear."

"All Fallon's men are probably handy with a gun." Tom's eyes were sweeping the plaza. "Fallon is making a move quicker than I thought he would."

"About an hour ago, Fallon's man was in the saloon buyin' a drink for your lady partner's brother," George said.

"Her brother's here?" Tom frowned at the news. "What's he like?"

Surprisingly, George Sell's serious features relaxed. "He's a young tomcat," said George, tolerantly. "Big young fellow. Good lookin'. Busts horses for ranches all over the Territory. Swaps horses too, an' races horses for bets. Crazy about fine horses, the man at the feed corral says. Likes his gamblin' too." A smile touched George Sell's stern mouth. "The world's his oyster, from what I hear. Young Bratton goes after it awhoopin'."

Tom had to smile himself. "He doesn't sound too bad."

Almost sheepishly, George admitted, "Makes a man hanker to get young and have a fling again. But don't take young Bratton careless. He's a hotheaded wildcat, quick to jump if he's crossed." George grew speculative. "I wonder why Fallon's man was sidin' him so close this mornin'? Young Bratton didn't look too happy."

"Trouble for us," Tom guessed, frowning.

George remembered something else, "Your new partner is buyin' supplies for a ranch crew."

"I bought supplies at the sutler's!" Tom said quickly. "Eagan is bringing them in the wagon."

"She's buyin' barrel flour, sack beans, lard, sowbelly slabs, an' plenty more," George said. "Who's she aimin' to feed at the ranch?"

"I'll ask her," Tom said angrily. "Which store is she in?"

FIVE

Virginia Bratton stepped out on the shady *portal* of the Frio Mercantile with her lightweight purchases stacked in her arms. Humming under her breath, she reached her buckboard at the hitchrack, and Tom Cantrell was standing in front of her, tall and unsmiling. She remembered his strong arms lifting her into the back of his wagon, and remarked coolly, "Judge Polk will be here in a few minutes."

Cantrell lifted her packages and put them in the buckboard. "Is the man really a judge?"

"Barnaby Polk was a judge admired by everyone," Virginia said with pride. "But he would rather practice law in Santa Fe. He's here to see me settled on the ranch."

Cantrell impassively regarded her blue dress with its gay red coral buttons. His remark was calmly businesslike, "I'd still like to buy Steve Rogers' half of the ranch."

"With a note?"

"Best I can do at this time."

"I'll not sell, even for cash," Virginia said. "I've arranged to buy my own cattle for my half of the ranch."

The dark angles of Cantrell's face hardened a little. "Who will handle your cattle?"

"I'm hiring my own crew."

"It won't work," he said. "Two crews in one bunkhouse won't work. Two cooks in one kitchen won't work. Two owners in one ranchhouse won't do."

"Rogers and his wife occupied half the ranchhouse," Virginia reminded him tartly. "I've hired a Mexican woman to live with me. My brother will be my foreman. We'll use our legal half of everything. Do as you wish with the other half."

Cantrell's dark face tightened. "Your brother will boss things?"

"Lee will boss our crew."

A smolder grew in Cantrell's eyes. "Steve Rogers was murdered, Miss Bratton. You've bought into a dead man's shoes. It can happen to your brother."

"We have nothing to do with that!"

Cantrell was deliberate. "I left the Army to start a ranch, which evidently isn't wanted in this unsettled part of the Territory. I've lost my partner, and men and money. From now on I'll call the trouble. This ranch will be bigger than Steve and I ever planned. And I'll break every man who tries to stop me!"

"If you're alive!" Virginia said coldly.

The corners of Cantrell's mouth quirked in a faint smile. For an instant he was likeable, even when his sarcasm followed: "That's something to look forward to."

"I never wish misfortune for anyone."

"I don't believe you do," Cantrell said, studying her, "but serious trouble is ahead. You don't belong in it."

"I want no part of it, Mr. Cantrell."

"You've bought into it, Miss Bratton. You should sell and get clear of it. Make no mistake; it will happen!"

Virginia was familiar with Lee's bursts of temper, which blazed quickly and were as quickly forgotten in Lee's reckless zest for life. This Tom Cantrell was different. His hard purpose was ominous as he watched her. Suddenly she was a little afraid of him.

"I don't frighten easily," Virginia said steadily. "The Judge will tell you my legal rights."

"You've been warned," Cantrell said.

Virginia looked past his tall figure and saw Lee riding to them. Cantrell turned. He stood motionless, watching Lee and Lee's horse. Virginia had seen other men transfixed as Cantrell was now, when Lee appeared on one of his prized horses.

This horse was a magnificent bay gelding, almost black, with a snowy face blaze and a pink lower lip. The horse's eyes were wide-set, alert; withers broad; haunches lean, powerful. Every silky hair had been lovingly groomed until the sun glinted from the burnished coat. Mincing sidewards to them on long tapering legs and small, light-stepping hoofs, the horse had a proud look of tremendous speed and endurance.

"What a pair!" Cantrell said under his breath, and Virginia wondered if she would ever completely dislike the man after his involuntary tribute to Lee.

The saddle and horsehair bridle were plain. There was no dandyish affectation about Lee. None was needed, Virginia thought with a catch of pride. Lee was superb, even in his plain denim pants and canvas jacket. Sitting straight up, molded to horse and saddle, Lee was completely confident of himself in a wild young way.

Lee swung a leg easily over the horse's neck and slid lithely off, dropping the looped reins over the saddle horn. He landed lightly, his right hand steadying his holstered gun, and pushed his hat back on his tousled black hair as he stepped up to them. The horse stood motionless, ears pricking after Lee.

Lee's expression made Virginia apprehensive. She had hoped these two men — Lee with his reckless temper and Cantrell with his hard strength — would not meet today. Reluctantly she said, "Mr. Cantrell — my brother, Lee Bratton."

"So this," Lee said, "is the partner?" and he did not offer his hand.

"I'm the partner," Cantrell said calmly. The hand he had meant to offer relaxed at his side. "You have a fine horse."

Lee's instinctive grin faded. "You're the man who lost Ginny's half of the Texas herd!" Lee pushed his hat farther back and looked Cantrell up and down.

They were about the same size; yet Cantrell's maturity gave the illusion that he was slightly taller and heavier. The thoughtful gravity in Cantrell's reply made Lee seem young and recklessly brash. "I'm that man," Cantrell agreed.

"I hear Indians maybe didn't get all your trail herd. A slick trick was worked on a girl you thought was helpless."

Disciplined control held Cantrell motionless, watching Lee. "That hardcase whom Matthew Fallon sent after us put the idea into your head, didn't he?" he asked, slowly.

"Matthew Fallon?" said Virginia. "Lee, isn't he the man you broke horses for?"

Cantrell regarded Lee more intently. "So," he said, "you worked for Fallon?"

"Who I've worked for is my business!" Lee said. "I get around. I hear things."

"A man fool enough to listen can hear anything. If he jumps when a man like Fallon pulls strings," Cantrell said, "he can find trouble fast."

Virginia had the helpless feeling of being trapped between these two big men, each so important in her life. Quickly she begged, "Lee, will you get the Judge?"

Lee's shoulders had pulled back stiffly. "Never mind the Judge! I'm here now!"

"I'll talk to the lawyer," Cantrell said. "Tell him, Miss Bratton, I'll be at the feed corral."

Lee moved closer. "Talk to me! My money's buying the cattle for Virginia's half of the ranch! I'm hiring the crew! I'll boss 'em! I'm not a helpless girl! Or an old man who'll be back in Santa Fe!"

"Don't play Matthew Fallon's game," Cantrell advised, quietly. "You've been fed lies to start trouble. And I don't want trouble with you."

"We'll talk about the herd! Ginny's half of the herd!"

"I'll talk with your sister; I'll discuss it with your lawyer," Cantrell said curtly. "But not you, buster!"

Lee hit him. Virginia gasped as Lee's hard fist smashed Cantrell's mouth, driving Cantrell reeling. And suddenly she had a strange feeling of triumph. She was not alone! Now Cantrell knew it! Then she remembered that they wore guns. She reached Lee's side and caught his arm.

"Stop it, Lee!"

Lee shook her off, and a hand caught her shoulder from behind. The Judge's grim voice said, "Keep out of this, Ginny!" He drew her back to the buckboard.

"They'll kill —"

"Cantrell," the Judge said, "is not a killer."

"But Lee —"

"Lee is not a killer — yet!" the Judge said. "Fools who dance must pay the fiddler. Lee must learn before some gunman kills him. Go into the store! Don't watch this!"

"No!" Virginia said. She was watching Tom Cantrell and she was desperately afraid.

Tom Cantrell was not afraid. Through dizzy shock Tom was thinking, *Fallon planned this too!* The warning of Major Alcorn followed: *"Someone will kill you!"*

This could be it; this young hothead egged into rage by the lies of Fallon's man. And Fallon himself once more out of sight, in the background, planning and maneuvering. Tom threw a dizzy look around for Fallon's gunman, or strangers who might be backing Lee Bratton.

Only the sister and the tall old lawyer stood beside the buckboard. Men were running toward the fight. Tom spat blood. He ducked Lee's next overeager swing and jumped back, circling while his head cleared.

Lee ran at him. Lee's slashing fist skidded off Tom's cheekbone, spinning him off balance again. Lee Bratton was big, strong and fast, with the bursting tide of youthful stamina and reckless confidence.

The Army tamed young roosters like this with sweat, drill and discipline, and they made the world's finest. But here was one who had never met discipline. And the sister had made this cocky, reckless young hothead a vital part of Tom Cantrell's whole future. Lee missed another furious swing and crowded close, strong and confident. He was dangerous. His bursting youth could wear down an older man. He could win this useless brawl; and if Lee did win, all the future would fall apart.

Tom realized how it would be. Lee Bratton's swaggering malice would dominate the ranch. The tale would spread far, giving confidence to dangerous men Tom Cantrell had to meet. Fallon's long-reaching enmity had made this unexpected hazard, which had to be quickly, ruthlessly beaten down. The opening Tom wanted was suddenly there. His long, looping blow struck tremendously, shockingly on Lee's nose.

In the crowd, someone yipped shrilly as Lee's head snapped back. Tom could feel the nose flatten under his slashing knuckles. Lee's big frame shuddered. But a bloody nose did little damage. Only to pride, to temper. Tom belted a left viciously into Lee's middle.

A gasp escaped Lee. And Tom drove his right fist again to the broken, bleeding nose. He slid away as Lee yelled thickly in pain and rage.

Lee swiped his hand over his nose. He glared at the red smear which came away, and charged in wild temper. A flailing fist struck Tom's chest. It was like being clubbed. Lee was breathing through his mouth. Whistling breaths sprayed red droplets from his streaming nose. Tom dodged another rush and stepped close as Lee swung around. His clubbing blow struck Lee off balance. Tom followed, sledging blows which beat Lee to his hands and knees in the churned dust.

Tom waited as Lee bounced up with another yell. Right fist smashed Lee's blood-smeared cheek. Left fist struck Lee's head bobbing. With brutal blows, Tom beat Lee staggering back against the close-packed spectators.

Great breaths shuddered from Lee's open mouth. The hands of strangers pushed him upright. All the high, reckless youth and temper had quickly been beaten into desperation.

A bearded teamster holding his coiled bull-whip called in heavy sarcasm to Lee, "Ye started hit! Whup 'im!"

Lee staggered forward.

Tom was drained and gasping too, but his explosive, *"Don't do it!"* came as Lee reached desperately under his canvas jacket for the gun holster there. Already Tom was lunging and grabbing to hamper Lee's gun wrist. And his right hand was pulling his own revolver.

Lee was dazed, slow. Tom whipped the gun up in a fast arc. The steel barrel struck Lee reeling. He fell hard, sprawling, scattering dust, rolling to his side.

Tom stood unsteadily over him, gun in hand. And in a swirl of her blue skirt, Virginia Bratton went to her knees in the dirt beside Lee. Tom heard her croon of pity over the smeared, beaten face. Then her aversion and fear came in a choking blaze as she looked up. "Have you killed him?"

"He'll live," Tom gasped from burning lungs. "Keep him away from me."

Sweat rolled down his face as he swung away from her, gun in hand. During the fight he had caught a blurred glimpse of the man named Joe Sloan, back in the crowd, expectantly grinning. Sweating, trying to get his breath, Tom looked for Fallon's man, who had started all this.

The close-crowding spectators stared back. Fallon's man was not among them now. Barnaby Polk, the tall old lawyer, stood beside the buckboard, remote and thoughtful, and a little sad. The old man seemed to be musing on what would follow this. And over the heads of the crowd, Tom saw Lieutenant Fitzpatrick watching him from the saddle. Fitz had brought his departing patrol close to the fight and halted. Now Fitz grinned at Tom's sweaty, panting figure.

"One of your easy, pleasant jobs?" Fitz called as his arm went up. Fitz's order to march rolled back along the column.

They passed on by twos, sun-blackened troopers grinning over as they went by. Tom Cantrell still was one of them, obviously, and they considered that the Army had won this skirmish against a civilian.

The crowd gave way silently as Tom shouldered through into the open. His glance swept the plaza. Fallon's man was not in sight. Tom started for the saloon on this side of the plaza, gun in hand.

He was breathing more easily when he reached the open doorway of the saloon and looked in.

The place was deserted, emptied by the fight.

George Sell's call reached Tom: "You want that one leavin' the feed corral?"

The quick pounding of a spurred horse's hoofs sounded from the west side of the plaza as Tom ran to the edge of the saloon *portal*. Fallon's man had ridden his horse out of the adobe-walled corral, and had seen Tom or heard George Sell. He spurred recklessly down into the trough of the Frio channel and up the opposite side, riding north. Tom holstered his gun with a shove and walked out to meet George Sell.

"He's heading back to Fallon," Tom said. "George, he started it by telling young Bratton we hid out most of the girl's cattle, instead of losing them."

George Sell, quiet and formidable when aroused, said, "Want me to go after him?"

"It's done now." Tom drew a sleeve over his wet face. "She's going to run her own cattle on the ranch. Have her own crew. Her brother will be her foreman."

George Sell looked startled. He lifted a hand to his sweeping brown mustaches, and after frowning a moment said quietly, "Not good."

They walked toward the feed corral, both of them reflective. "There'll be more of Fallon," Tom said. And when George nodded agreement, Tom said briefly, "We'll go to the ranch and get ready."

SIX

New Mexico Territory was an immense, sun-drenched, empty land, yet news could race across the far horizons. The man named Joe Sloan rode north, pushing his long-striding gray gelding. Lieutenant Fitzpatrick's patrol carried word of the furious fight to the Fort Ross garrison. And a buckboard carrying the mails rolled south, its driver musing over the fight he had witnessed.

Far south, the deep-dug well of the Lobo Flat relay station held the only sweet water in parched miles of mesquite and cactus. Sunset laced the western sky with scarlet streamers as six rangy Texans on tired horses, and leading two pack horses, reached the Lobo station from the south. Night was falling when a dusty stage from the south swung into the walled yard of the station. Minutes later the mail buckboard rattled in from the north.

The six Texans had the feral look of dangerous brush cats as they took seats at the station's long plank supper table and ate wolfishly, ignoring others. But the mail driver's account of the fight in the Frio Plaza was abruptly interrupted by the Texan opposite him.

"The name, suh, was Cantrell?" the Texan drawled over the thick antelope steak he had been demolishing.

"Tom Cantrell."

"Back from Texas with a herd?"

"Back with nary a nubby steer," said the mail driver. "Lost his herd and half his crew."

Knife in one hand, fork in the other, the Texan chewed reflectively. His shirt was buckskin without fringing. A brace of long-barreled revolvers, and a long bone-handled knife in a leather sheath well back on his left hip, seemed a casual part of him. The driver had noticed such things when this Texan had washed his face and hands outside, and used his broken half of a comb on his yellow mustache and long yellow hair. Thereafter this man had drawn apart, rangy and silent, with restless eyes watching every movement in the walled yard.

Thoughtfully the Texan's polite drawl persisted, "This Cantrell's got a ranch?"

"Call it a ranch," the driver said, humorously. "All he needs is cattle on it." The driver waited expectantly for more questions, which did not come as the Texan silently attacked his food again.

And in this same sunset the man named Joe Sloan, far north of the Frio Plazas, spurred his exhausted gray gelding up a shallow canyon of the Secundos, to an isolated adobe hut with a small corral alongside which held three horses.

A Mexican hurried out of the hut and helped switch the saddle to a fresh horse. A silent, dark-faced woman brought wheat tortillas and a tin plate of meat chunks laced with fiery red chili. Sloan ate ravenously, hardly speaking. He rolled a smoke, swung onto the fresh horse, and the inky night swallowed him as he rode on. When he met the blaze of the next morning's sunrise, Sloan was through the Secundos, heading east through a tremendous country of long ridges, colorful buttes and hidden, canyon-like valleys.

Hours later Sloan followed a faint trail through black brush, and down red rock steeps into a valley running sinuously southeast between red and yellow rock sides. A glint of water wandered through the middle of the valley between silvery-gray chamiso thickets. After a time grazing cattle appeared. Finally tall cotton-woods lifted ahead and the temporary Largo Canyon camp was there.

A weathered wagon with a chuck box built in the back stood by the cottonwoods. A sooty coffee pot rested on smoking embers. Bedrolls were scattered on the ground. Ropes stretched between the cottonwoods corraled horses. And Matthew Fallon, standing beside the wagon with several men, recognized the approaching rider and walked out to meet him.

Fallon had not been under a roof since he had first encountered Tom Cantrell. His expanding interests kept him moving over all this vast, unclaimed wild country, where only the strong dominated. The war had spun him off, bitter and unwanted, his health gone and his right hand forever useless. He had built this new life with only superior intelligence and ruthlessness. The claw of a right hand, which he regarded every day with revulsion, had driven him like an excoriating demon. Without a gun hand, he had found health, profit and power; and the power meant most. He got an immense feeling of satisfaction when men with two perfect hands jumped to his bidding. Matthew Fallon's name was important, even among savage tribes which looted and slaughtered most whites. And now Tom Cantrell threatened everything that Matthew Fallon valued.

"Is Cantrell dead?" he called out. He realized it sounded too eager for a man who tried to present a jaunty confidence to all men.

The rider did not notice. He was too tired. "I took a chance you'd still be at the camp here. That Cantrell beat the hell out of Lee Bratton in the Upper Frio Plaza yesterday."

"Young Bratton at the Frio?"

"Got there yesterday mornin'." Sloan dismounted stiffly and stood a moment, working his cramped shoulders. He grinned wearily. "I got in my talk before Lee seen Cantrell."

"What talk?"

Fallon listened intently as Sloan told him. Part of Fallon's mind jumped back, as it did constantly these days, to Cantrell's arrival in the country. A man sent surreptitiously to Cantrell with an offer of cheap cattle and horses for the new ranch had been rebuffed by Cantrell with cold temper. No stock, nor any man connected with the Comanche trade would be on the new ranch or near it, Cantrell had warned. It had been threat and challenge, even though Matthew Fallon's name had not been mentioned to Cantrell.

Joe Sloan was saying, "No young hellion like Lee Bratton'll forget a beating like Cantrell give him yesterday. Next time Lee won't try fists."

Fallon's thoughts went back to the first try he'd made against Cantrell. Dropping everything, he had followed Cantrell to Texas, to block the man before Cantrell dug in near the Frio with his first trail herd. And in Texas he had discovered Cantrell was using his crew to gather legal claims to stolen stock.

Joe Sloan said, "Cantrell don't want Lee Bratton's sister for a new partner. They've had words. Lee has throwed in with his sister."

Fallon drew a slow breath. Cantrell's herd was gone. Cantrell's first partner was dead. But Cantrell himself loomed astride the Frio country, more threatening than ever.

"Lee Bratton said he was heading north to Las Vegas. He'll hire a crew, an' buy cattle and horses for their half of the ranch."

"A crew of his own?" said Fallon. "On the ranch with Cantrell? After Cantrell beat him bloody?" He stood thinking about it. "Did you tell Lee about that yellow-gold horse with a white mane and tail?"

"Made his eyes shine. He'll come by the ranch on his way to Las Vegas."

"You've earned an extra hundred dollars," Fallon said impulsively. "Get some rest, and follow me to the Gallinas ranch."

Fallon knew cynically that men like Joe Sloan stayed at heel only while money came easily. But Sloan had earned this gift. Lee Bratton could be handled. For Cantrell this was the beginning of the end.

Far south toward the Frio, it was Eagan's warning shout which rang through the wide ranch yard: "She's bringin' gunmen with her!"

Tom Cantrell stood motionless in the small adobe saddle shed, remembering the gun Lee Bratton had tried to draw. Reluctantly Tom checked his own revolver before he stepped outside.

South, where the rough ruts from the Frio Plazas lifted out of a wide, grassy draw, three wagons and a number of riders were in sight. The boy had been examining Eagan's big revolver. Eagan was reaching for the weapon. George Sell was coming purposefully from the corral. Pete Yancey shouldered out of the bunkhouse, cocking a carbine.

"No guns!" Tom called.

Bareheaded, the sleeves of his old blue military blouse rolled back, Tom walked forward

73

and watched the groaning four-horse wagons approach. Virginia Bratton and the old lawyer were riding ahead. Lee Bratton was not in sight.

Wind stirred the Bratton girl's long straw-colored skirt as she sat the sidesaddle lightly. Her small red hat looked gay in the sunlight. She hardly reached his shoulder, Tom remembered. Her blue eyes and fair skin were unusual with such black hair. When she had knelt in the plaza dirt beside her brother, her anger and aversion had been a choking blaze.

She seemed calm now as she wheeled her horse back. Tom heard her call, "First wagons to the back of the house! Last wagon to the front!" She knew he was standing there and she rode toward the front of the house, ignoring him.

The old lawyer rode up to Tom. "Young man, I find no basis in the suggestion that Indians did not take your trail herd." Under his breath, the old man added, *"Experientia docet stultos!"*

Tom put the words into dry English: " 'Experience teaches fools!' " He added more dryly, "Who gets the experience? Are those gunmen the teachers?"

Barnaby Polk looked surprised, then detached and unconcerned as he turned his horse toward the corral. "They joined us a few miles back," he said as he moved away. "They have asked questions and told nothing."

Tom gazed toward the armed strangers with new interest, and walked to meet them. One rider advanced. "Yo' name Cantrell?" a polite drawl inquired.

The man had long yellow hair and a yellow mustache. He was not much past thirty, Tom decided. The plain leather shirt and two long revolvers were on a rangy, sinewy frame.

"I'm Cantrell," Tom said. "How's Texas?"

The reply was a cool drawl, "Bleedin' from Comanche raids. Damn-yanks all over the place, reconstructin' folks. I'm Ashley Hampton." He stepped down with catlike litheness. His reserved glance estimated Tom.

"Passing through?" Tom inquired.

"All depends," the polite drawl said. "You the man who was gatherin' power-of-attorney papers in Texas?"

SEVEN

"What papers?" Tom said with his own reserve.

Ashley Hampton drawled, "Folks spoke well of you in Texas. Old Will Seabright, near Five Springs, said he gave you power of attorney coverin' his JV brand, that Comanches had raided bad. There was talk you'd welcome help."

"I need help," Tom said, "but only from men interested in recovering stolen Texas cattle. Not from Texans fired-up to raid damn-yanks. Or wild ones who won't take orders."

"I gave orders in the war," Ashley Hampton said coolly. "I can take orders from the right man."

"Who are your friends?"

"All of us from the same county. Rode the war together. Been down in Chihuahua an' didn't like it. Ridin' north, we heard yo' name mentioned and stopped by."

If the other five strangers were like this one, they were not a breed to be working for Matthew Fallon, Tom decided. He made a tentative decision: "There's the bunkhouse; make yourselves at home. We'll talk it over." His glance went to the loaded wagons. "This ranch has two owners. My men and I are the only ones here interested in stolen Texas stock."

The Texan regarded the loaded wagons gravely. He knew, undoubtedly, about the fight with Lee Bratton. He might be aware of the clashing emotions involved in the Bratton girl's taking over her half of the ranch. No hint of it was in the Texan's comment: "A man can't be too cautious when fightin' is ahead."

Something like a glint of humor came into the Texan's gray eyes as he turned to his horse. His remark could have had several meanings. Tom's own humor warmed his reserve as he watched the Texan beckon to his companions and lead his horse toward the bunkhouse.

But when George Sell walked over, Tom said, "They're Texas men. See if they ring sound, George, before I make any decisions."

And as he walked to the house, Tom thought soberly of Major Alcorn's warning. Texas men, helping Tom Cantrell recover stolen Texas stock, would bring Alcorn and his troops into any trouble. Alcorn was a man of his word. Yet without help from Texas, Tom's future on this empty new ranch was hopeless. When Tom thought about it, his anger came again. He put decisions aside now, and watched what was happening to his home.

Wiry Mexican men from the Lower Plaza had driven the wagons. Virginia Bratton had brought furniture and personal effects. She was moving in with her treasures, calmly making her own nest, no matter whom she crowded out.

In the kitchen, Tom had to step aside as two Mexicans staggered in with a heavy leather trunk. A moment later the old lawyer stepped in, removed his high hat, and glanced around with interest. And then had to move quickly aside himself as two more Mexicans lurched in with a large feather mattress. *Feathers!* Not even Steve Rogers' bride had brought feathers.

Shrewd lines deepened at the corners of Barnaby Polk's blue eyes as he noted Tom's darkening look. "After the storm, the sunshine, young man," the old lawyer said, smiling a little.

Tom looked at him without humor. "When will Lee Bratton be here?"

The old lawyer frowned. "I've ordered Lee to stay away for a long time," Barnaby Polk said. He placed his tall hat on the kitchen table. "You seem to have built well here."

"My partner and I had plans." It was difficult to resent this benign, tall old man. "I'll show you the house," Tom offered.

He and Steve Rogers had been proud of this massive, adobe headquarters, which was not yet finished. They had built a side wing for each of them, with a huge living room between. Peeled logs held up the low ceilings. Dirt twenty inches deep covered the flat roof. Floors were of hard-dried, puddled adobe mud, until lumber would be easier to get.

They had run back high side walls enclosing a spacious patio. Across the back they had put kitchen, eating room, storeroom, cook's room. Against possible siege, a second well had been dug in the patio. The house was a fort, with small windows and heavy shutters. And now this Virginia Bratton owned half!

They met her small, busy figure. Her preoccupied smile flashed for the old lawyer and ignored Tom. A plump Mexican woman — Doña Sarina, Tom heard the Bratton girl call her — bustled about vigorously in an enveloping apron of violent-hued flower pattern, scolding the native men in bursts of liquid Spanish.

Life had filled this house when Steve and his bride had been in it. The thick-walled rooms had held laughter, gaiety, love and enthusiasm. Tom had returned from Texas to the lonely aftermath of grief, from which Steve's wife had fled back to her tidewater Maryland. Now life filled the house again, brisk and purposeful.

They returned to the kitchen. Barnaby Polk offered his black leather cigar case. Tom accepted one of the villainous cheroots.

Thoughtfully, Barnaby Polk said, "You have an establishment. Ginny Bratton was fortunate in her purchase." The lines at his shrewd blue eyes deepened again as his glance considered Tom. "It should be possible to endure this partnership without friction."

They both had to move quickly out of the way as four Mexican men staggered in with a walnut organ. Tom watched this ultimate in feminine domesticity vanish toward the front of the house.

"It should be possible," Tom conceded, but there was no conviction in his voice as he thought of the stubborn girl and her hotheaded brother, here in the house, squarely in the midst of his own life and plans.

At Fort Ross, Major Alcorn sat at his desk in the small headquarters building, and chewed the frayed end of his cigar while Adjutant Blount waited silently.

A trooper, posted for desertion, had been found back in the hills, his head sliced off like a turnip top and wedged in the crook of his stiffened arm, as if the unlucky man were desperately retaining his separated part. A foul sense of humor, these Apaches!

Alcorn could think of worse they'd done, and would do. He took the cigar from his mouth. "There's some doubt the fellow did desert. We'll bury him properly and straighten out his record."

"Yes, sir."

Before Adjutant Blount could leave, Alcorn spoke thoughtfully, "Any more news about Tom Cantrell?"

"Not since Cantrell's fight with the girl's brother, sir."

"Very well."

Alone, Alcorn ran his fingers through his

shock of graying blond hair. Under his breath he muttered a heartfelt cavalryman's oath. At Fort Union, for a time, there had seemed some slight possibility that Tom Cantrell might end up in the family.

Alcorn doubted it now as he looked at his daughter's framed photograph on top of the desk. Isabel's assured smile told him exactly nothing. But Tom Cantrell's gaunt, angry face the other night had held promise of what was going to happen soon.

Cantrell was the man to do it. He would take armed Texans through the country like a destructive scythe. Make a shambles of peace and order. Worse, Cantrell would be right; and the man at this desk would have to stop it, no matter how he felt. Alcorn felt gloomy and annoyed as his thoughts jumped to the boy that Cantrell had picked up. And to the boy's mother, held by the same sort of Apaches who had caught the deserter and no doubt thoroughly enjoyed his frantic screams before tiring of the sport.

Nothing practical could be done at this time about the boy's mother. Alcorn caught himself glancing at Isabel's picture and wondering — almost guiltily — what he'd do if Isabel were held by the same Apaches.

He suspected what he'd do, and swore again under his breath as he bent to the reports on his desk. That small boy and mother would stay on his mind, Alcorn knew.

Isabel Alcorn was thinking about Tom Cantrell when she met Adjutant Blount near the post hospital. Archie Blount was a young man of energy who fancied himself; he caught off his garrison cap and might have been aware of her thoughts.

"I wonder," Adjutant Blount said expansively — and knowingly, "if Tom Cantrell would be interested in a report about his former partner that the sergeant-major ran across in the files?"

"Why ask me?" Isabel said calmly.

Adjutant Blount half-closed a knowing eye, decided not to pursue the matter, and said, "A patrol from the garrison we relieved found the body of Cantrell's partner. The sheriff's office being over a hundred miles away, the lieutenant put all the facts he could find into his report."

A quick thought speeded Isabel's pulses. She had wanted some reasonable excuse to visit Tom Cantrell at his new ranch. Her smiling request made Archie Blount a co-conspirator in a way. "Can I have a copy of the report, Archie?"

Adjutant Blount beamed. "Have it for you tomorrow."

Isabel walked on to the hospital building, already planning the visit. And it put her thoughts again on the Bratton girl, at the ranch every day now with Tom. Isabel frowned and tried not to think about it.

It was evening when Virginia Bratton relaxed in her bedroom, cross-legged in a wooden tub of water, her hair caught up in a towel. The gourd dipper in Doña Sarina's brown hand cascaded cold water over her bare neck and shoulders.

"C-C-o-o-ld!" Virginia gasped. "The towel, Sarina!"

Wrapped in the towel, Virginia sat and looked contentedly about the lamplit room. Her own walnut spool bed, fetched all the way from Santa Fe. Her walnut bureau with French-plate oval mirror. Her walnut lowboy, with Lee's smiling photograph on top. Bright chintz curtains over the window and closed shutters, through which seeped the yapping clamor of coyotes in the near night.

Virginia drew a satisfied breath. "Home, Sarina!"

Doña Sarina spoke in Spanish. "This house of strange men! And only we two women! Who," said Doña Sarina darkly, "knows what?"

Someone knocked on the heavy plank door. Doña Sarina made the sign of the cross over her ample bosom. Virginia chuckled, and called from the tub, "Yes?"

The Judge's genial voice spoke through the door. "Too tired, Ginny, to play the organ for us this evening?"

"For those men?"

"It would be nice."

Virginia sat in frowning, stubborn silence. The Judge's mild voice coaxed, "For me then, Ginny? Your first night in a new home should be a happy one."

"Of course, if you want me to," Virginia said.

He was a wise old man. His purpose was plain. Warmth under this roof — even if friendliness were impossible — might be best for her and Lee. Especially Lee. Virginia stood up in the tub, toweling herself.

"I think the black challis skirt and the pink basque," she said, in reflective Spanish. "And my red-and-yellow gold earrings."

"For *Tejanos!*" Doña Sarina muttered.

Virginia laughed as she stepped from the tub to the thick rag rug on the hard mud floor. Her life had been encompassed by such rough men. She understood their great strengths and violent weaknesses, from which most of them rallied sheepishly.

She got dressed, and then, with the small glass lamp glowing beside the mirror, she lightly used chamois skin backed with flannel and filled with face powder. A twirl before the mirror flipped the long red-and-yellow gold earrings against her neck. She opened the door and walked into the living room. And heard Doña Sarina take a watchful position in the open doorway behind her.

EIGHT

Bracket lamps glowed on the lime-washed walls of the long living room. Firelight from blazing cedar chunks in the big stone fireplace danced over the men who stared silently at her. They seemed to fill the room — big men, booted and spurred, wearing cartridge belts and guns. The Judge, tall and dignified in his black suit, beamed at her like a pleased conspirator. Tom Cantrell stood tall, gaunt and unsmiling, at the far end of the fireplace. In his own half of the living room, Virginia noted.

The Judge said, "Ginny, this is a great favor to us all."

"The fire," Virginia said, smiling, "looks so cheerful." The small boy stood there, solemnly regarding her. Virginia went to him and put her hand lightly on his shoulder. He moved away.

Smiling, the Judge indicated the wide Axminster carpet on the dried-mud floor. "Even carpet."

"Mrs. Rogers brought this carpet from Maryland, for her new home," Virginia said. She knelt down and ran her palm lightly over the bright colors. "A little of her far-away Maryland under-foot, in this wild country which seemed empty and dangerous to her." Virginia straightened soberly. "And it did take her man and her happiness."

Cantrell spoke coolly from his end of the fireplace. "Evidently you have no such fears."

"I was reared in the Territory," Virginia said, quite as coolly. "I find it friendly — mostly."

The walnut organ was at her end of the long room. The Judge brought a wall lamp as Virginia adjusted the stool. The silent Texans, she was thinking, were as formidable a group as she had ever seen. What were they doing here? Casually, without looking around, she said, "Eddy, don't you want to stand by me while I play?" When she sat down, the small silent boy sidled close.

"What shall I try first?" Virginia asked over her shoulder.

A lean Texan impulsively said, "You know 'Dixie,' ma'am?"

Quiet fell as Virginia started to play. Then the rich baritone of the Texan named Ashley Hampton caught up the words. Others joined in. And as the singing gained volume, Virginia noticed that all the Texans were unobtrusively shifting position behind her. They were gathering around Ashley Hampton, at her right.

Standing together, the massed ardor of their voices lifted, wild and a little frightening. And at the end, a fierce, challenging Rebel yell rang through the room.

Virginia looked up uncertainly at the red, grim face of Cantrell's man, Eagan, at the left side of the organ. Eagan had started to sing the great, moving marching song of the North: "The Battle Hymn of the Republic."

This should be amusing, Virginia thought uneasily as she caught it up with the organ. But the deep passions of the late war lurked in all these men. Eagan's singing grew in force. Cantrell's voice, back of her, joined in. And his men. There was little enthusiasm from the Texans now.

Virginia let them have their second verse: *"I have seen Him in the watchfires of a hundred circling camps —"* And then she struck a discordant chord, and softly began to play and sing, *"Should auld acquaintance be forgot —"*

With relief, she heard Cantrell join her. Did he sound a little amused? All the men sang, some of them sounding slightly sheepish, and passion drained from the room. At the end a Texan said, pensively, "My mother used to sing 'Rock of Ages' to us kids —"

Virginia saw the small boy at her elbow dip his head and close his eyes. "How about 'De Camptown Races'?" she said quickly, and started the merry tune. But the damage was done.

The boy was silently moving back behind the men. When Virginia looked around, he was slipping out into the dark patio. Small and alone! Her impulse was to follow. Then Virginia saw the stolid Eagan following the boy into the patio. She turned to the organ, feeling better.

Finally she swung around, smiling up at the half-circle of rough men. They grinned back at her. Only Cantrell's dark face was unmoved.

"We're leaving in the morning," Cantrell said. "There are several things you and I should discuss, Miss Bratton."

"We can step outside; I'll get a shawl," Virginia said.

In her bedroom, from a drawer of the lowboy, she took her prized India shawl of filmy black cashmere, with exotic designs in silver and gold thread. Her glance stopped on Lee's photograph on top of the lowboy. All of Lee's bursting, youthful confidence grinned at her. Who would have thought, when this picture was made in Santa Fe, that she would go to her knees in a remote plaza of the Territory, frantically wiping blood from Lee's ferociously beaten face? Or that Lee, lurching on weak legs in the kitchen of her rented house, washing caked blood from his features, would be so deathly quiet? Even the Judge, watching from a chair, had seemed deeply troubled. They had never seen fury so tightly coiled, so silent in Lee.

Sober, troubled, Virginia was still thinking of Lee when the front door closed behind her and Cantrell. They walked out into the velvety starlight. Cantrell loomed beside her in his faded blue military blouse, open at the neck. His slow steps crunched, his spurs chinked softly. He sounded grudging when he spoke.

"I can't take the boy along. Will you keep him?"

"Of course."

The vastness of the empty country had closed about them. Coyotes clamored to the massed stars. Cantrell's voice sounded uncompromising. "Is your brother still planning to bring cattle and a crew on this ranch?"

Thinking again of his savage handling of Lee, Virginia said coldly, "What business is it of yours, Mr. Cantrell? Have I asked what these Texans are doing here? Or where you are riding tomorrow?"

"No," Cantrell admitted.

"Half this ranch —"

"Half is yours," he cut in dryly. "But I've had a sample of your brother. I don't want any more trouble with him."

"I don't want trouble!" Virginia said.

They had strolled beyond the house, and turned back and stopped. The stars, almost brilliant enough to read by, struck glints from the gold and silver threads in her shawl. Westward, the great bulk of the Lizard Butte lifted darkly. The thick walls of the house seemed to dominate the infinity of distance about them.

All this is mine! quickened in Virginia's thoughts. *My land! My home! . . . Half of it, anyway!*

She could visualize it, wild, empty, lonely, with fierce Apaches lurking in the dark mountains to the south. That unfortunate bride from Maryland had feared all that stretched out, lonely and empty, in this night. And she had been wrong!

The rich promising future, as the Judge had wisely said, was rooted in this immense new ranch. Every vibrant inch came alive as Virginia stood beside Cantrell's tall figure and thought about it. Cantrell's arms had been hard, ruthless when they had lifted her into the back of his wagon. She resented him. But he was strong enough, ruthless enough, to take this wild land and make it his own. She sensed it now.

"This new ranch is not wanted here," Cantrell's even voice said. "I believe I was followed to Texas. My men were killed, my herd was taken, my partner was murdered while I was gone. The Apaches can't be trusted. Being a woman won't make you safe."

"I will not sell or leave," Virginia said quietly.

Laughing voices lifted at the back of the house — men heading toward the bunkhouse. "I'm beginning to believe you," Cantrell said. He sounded bitter.

In silence they returned to the house. Firelight still danced across the long, empty living room. Doña Sarina waited watchfully in the bedroom doorway. They stopped in front of the fireplace. Cantrell's sober gaze touched her black hair, gay pink basque and black skirt. The light wavered across his dark, big-boned face as he looked back into the fireplace. Reverie held him.

"Good night," he said abruptly. His spurs chinked across the carpet. His own bedroom door closed behind him.

A housewifely thought quirked humor on Virginia's mouth. He had forgotten that lamps must be put out. Manlike, he had left it to the woman. "Sarina," Virginia said, "we'll put out the lamps."

In the morning, horses were outside her window, trampling, bucking as they unkinked in the first run from the corral. Virginia sat up in bed, pushing back her hair, listening.

Cantrell and his men were leaving. The massed drumming of hoofs swept by her open window and pounded into distance. She wondered again where they were going. Cantrell had no cattle, no money; yet he was riding away with bold, dangerous men.

At Matthew Fallon's ranch on the Gallinas, a note of wild defiance screamed in the bugling challenge of the golden horse as Lee Bratton walked to the corral bars. Matthew Fallon's crippled hand tightened in his coat pocket as sullen moroseness vanished from Lee's bruised face. Challenge leaped visibly in Lee.

"Arabian in him," Lee said. A smiling, dreamy look caught him as the powerful, neat-looking horse wheeled into a run which half-circled the big corral, and faced them again. Sunlight gleamed on the burnished golden coat and the snowy mane and tail. Another defiant bugle challenged them.

Casually, Fallon asked, "Ever see a finer horse?"

"Comanche-stole, out of Texas," Lee guessed, without taking his eyes off the horse.

"No brand on him," Fallon said indifferently.

"He was stole," said Lee, faintly contemptuous. "Like that horse Cantrell took from you."

Fallon's smile whitened at the corners. "I bought that roan gelding in good faith. When Cantrell claimed him, I didn't argue."

"That's not the way Cantrell's men told it in the Upper Frio Plaza." A jeer came into Lee's tone. "They were laughing over how Cantrell made the fellow with the crooked hand hop on another horse and get going."

The anger which tore Fallon in a great tide made him a little sick. His twisted, useless hand mocked before saloon drunks! And by this swaggering young hothead, who stood two inches taller than Matthew Fallon, both his hands strong and whole! And all the rest of him as wild and irresponsible as the big golden brute in the corral! *How Cantrell had mauled Lee's face!*

Breathing softly, Fallon looked vindictively at the mashed-looking nose, the dark bruises still puffy on Lee's cheekbones. But his warning was casual: "Two men who tried to ride this horse were half-killed."

Lee took the bait. "They didn't know their business. I can ride any horse."

92

"You're not over the beating Cantrell gave you," Fallon said, maliciously.

Lee's glower showed memory of the fight still clawing white-hot and deep. *He's powder, ready to blow,* Fallon decided with satisfaction. "Make the ride," he suggested, "and we'll trade. You're heading to Las Vegas to hire a crew and buy cattle and horses. Why go there? Everything you need is here."

"Comanche-stole out of Texas! Gun jumpers on the dodge!" Lee was contemptuous.

"The Comanches have traded cattle and horses into New Mexico for fifty years," Fallon said. "All I've done is put the trade on a businesslike basis."

"Wish I had a dollar for every Mexican Comanch' trader you've crowded out, had shot or frightened off," Lee said. "You think the Mexicans don't talk behind their hands about you? Anybody gets in your way, you take care of him!"

"I can't stop talk," Fallon said, shrugging. "I'm a trader, making money for myself and the men who trade with me. I'll sell you more cattle and horses for your money than you'll get anywhere else. And you can hire a crew here cheaper."

Lee's gaze was still on the horse in the corral. A slow grin of anticipation spread on his bruised face. "He's a beauty!" he said, drawing a breath. "I'll get my saddle."

NINE

Lee had the brash look of youth, lean-hipped and confident as he carried saddle, bridle and rope into the corral. The big yellow horse watched him. *Two wild ones!* Matthew Fallon thought.

Extra men Fallon had brought in to this home ranch on the Gallinas were drifting to the corral. They watched silently as Lee shook out his rope and moved forward. The big yellow-gold horse stood with head high, immovable, even when the loop snaked over his neck. It struck Fallon that the horse had a humanly intelligent look of waiting. Intently he watched Lee swiftly bridle and saddle the horse without using blindfold, foot rope or snubbing post.

Lee removed the rope. His sinewy body flipped into the saddle. Suddenly without warning, the horse tried to kill. A snake-like lunge whipped Lee's body violently before his feet were set in the stirrups. A bugling, defiant scream filled the corral as the big horse flung up and back on hind legs, intending plainly to hurtle over backwards and crash down on the rider. Fallon's crippled hand strained in his coat pocket as the great golden horse went straight up on its hind legs, its mouth open, its nostrils red and wide, its snowy mane and tail streaming in the sunlight.

Lee had mounted without a quirt. Instead of trying to twist off to safety, Lee yelled with joyous exuberance. Riding the almost perpendicular horse, in the instant before hurtling over backward, Lee struck his clenched fist tremendously behind the horse's ears. And struck again, almost too fast to follow.

Later, the men around Fallon argued that the horse must have changed his mind. No man could strike that hard with a bare fist. But the horse went forward again, leaping, twisting in the air before landing on stiff legs with a bone-snapping jar.

Instantly it was in the air again in another violent whirl. Lee swayed dangerously and barely stayed on. The horse lunged across the corral in bone-jarring pitches, ending in another whirl. Then a tremendous pitch, a dizzying swapping of ends as he soared up again.

Lee had stopped smiling. His lithe body whipped and snapped. Blood started from his nose. His hat dropped off. His black hair fell over his eyes. A grim, fierce exaltation filled him.

Lee had left the corral gate open. He yelled suddenly and spurred for the first time. The horse bucked toward the gate and bolted out of the corral, across the ranch yard toward open range.

An eighth of a mile out the wild, skimming run whirled off another spasm of bucking. Then the run took up again, toward the nearest low hills, and vanished from sight.

"Somebody better ride after him," a man near Fallon warned. "That devil won't stop 'til the saddle's empty! He'll scrape Bratton off in the brush, or throw him!"

"Two of you go!" Fallon ordered. He wished now he hadn't allowed this. Only a sound, strong Lee Bratton, hating Cantrell, was of use to him.

Two men spurred off toward the hills and disappeared. Fallon left the corrals and entered his square-built stone house. It was a small house, indifferently furnished. He was usually away, moving over the vast, empty land.

Alone, Fallon tossed his brown straw sombrero on a hide chair and drew the clawlike right hand from his coat pocket. He wore suits, always, so a coat pocket could conceal this derisive affliction. But in the Upper Frio Plaza Cantrell's men had laughed about this hand. Lee Bratton had laughed, too. Fallon lighted a cigar and paced the floor, thinking about it in shame and fury.

He was standing in the back doorway of the house almost an hour later, irritably smoking a second cigar, when one of the men shouted from the bunkhouse steps and pointed.

Lee Bratton had vanished among the low hills to the south. He was returning from the west. The big yellow horse was still running, its white

96

mane and tail streaming.

The horse's golden coat was flecked with gray foam. Its nostrils flared wide. Lee ran the horse through the open gate of the corral, pulled up and swung down. And staggered.

"Help him!" Fallon ordered sharply.

Lee's harsh, strained voice came back: "Keep away!"

Lee jerked the latigos free, hauled off the saddle and bridle, and turned to the gate with lurching steps. Like a man half dead, Fallon thought. Lee had bled from the nose and mouth, and smeared the blood with the back of a hand.

He stumbled through the open gate on stiff, numb-looking legs, and turned and looked at the horse. Lee's drawn, smeared face was grinning when Fallon joined him.

"Come to the house and have a drink," Fallon said.

The look Lee turned on him was hot and exultant. "I'll ride Cantrell like this!" he said fiercely.

When the two of them were alone in the house, Fallon watched the blazing emotion drive Lee in jerky strides over the wide, rough-sawed planks of the parlor floor. Lee held a second drink of whiskey, forgotten for the moment. Standing by the table, Fallon held his own untasted whiskey and spoke casually.

"You can have the horse cheap. But what about cattle and other horses you'll need? And a crew?"

"Comanch-stole cattle!"

Calmly logical, Fallon said, "You're hot to buy a Comanche-traded horse. What's the difference in buying cattle too?"

Lee swung around at the end of the room. Blood, started by the furious ride, was oozing again from his smashed nose. He yanked a blue bandana from his hip pocket, patted his nose and malignantly regarded the cloth.

Coolly Fallon prodded, "You'll need good men when you get home, or you'll jump to Cantrell's orders. He'll be at you again."

"When I go on that ranch with my herd and a crew," Lee said in a low voice, "Cantrell will jump!"

"You'd better have a crew that Cantrell can't bluff. Men like I've got outside," Fallon said. He watched Lee as Lee considered the proposition. Idly he suggested, "If something should happen to Cantrell, you'd end up with all that big ranch."

Lee nodded. "Old Barnaby Polk is lawyer enough to see to that."

"You can have the horse. I'll sell you a mixed herd at five dollars a head. You'll never buy that cheap again."

Lee's grin came thin and jeering. "After Cantrell made you hop off a horse, you'd lose money to get your own gunmen on Cantrell's ranch, inside his guard."

"I'm a businessman," Fallon said. "More cattle are coming in from the Plains than I can use right now. I need cash money. You've got cash, I suppose?"

"I've got authority to draft against my own money in Santa Fe, which Barnaby Polk holds in trust."

"That's more than good. How many men would you need?"

Lee calculated for a moment. "Cantrell lost half his men coming from Texas. Has four men left. No money, no cattle. He'll probably fire one or two of the men he has. With five or six men, I can run him off the ranch."

"I'll give you bills of sale for range delivery," Fallon said. "You can take men from here and meet the cattle coming in from the Plains. Cull them as close as you like. After that, you're on your own — if you think you can handle Cantrell."

"Handle him? I'll —" Lee drew a breath and drained his whiskey glass. "I guess there's no difference between the horse and your cattle," he conceded. "Might as well get all I can for my money."

"Other men have," Fallon said.

The small canyon in the Horse Hills where Tom Cantrell stood sipping hot coffee from a tin cup was a hundred and twenty-five miles north of the Frio. His men and the Texans had scattered out when they left the ranch. On a front more than a hundred miles wide they had moved north. Rendezvous was in this isolated canyon where a shallow little stream roiled out of the high hills, and the white limestone cliffs were topped by pines and rugged cedars which seemed to brush the blue sky. Half an hour ago the last of the Texans had ridden in. All the Texans, Tom noted, were more sober than when they had left the ranch.

"We'll decide here," Tom said deliberately.

His saddle and his leather saddle bags were on the ground near the small campfire. He left the tin cup by the saddle and returned with two small leather-bound tally books and two tin cylinders with waterproof caps.

The Texans were watching him closely. Tom ran a look over them. "I've waited, because I can't use any man who'll get faint-hearted and back out. Once this starts, the country will be boiling. Strangers can run. I have a ranch to hold. Only men who'll take orders and stay to the end will do."

Ashley Hampton, the tall Texan with yellow hair and mustache, drawled quietly, "Are you man enough to do what you think you can do?"

Tom eyed the rangy figure in leather shirt, with long, holstered revolvers. Hampton evidently had been an officer in the war, although he had not said. By tacit consent, Hampton seemed to speak for the other five Texans. Tom said, "I'm man enough to keep going until I'm stopped. I wanted you men to see what's in the country. When everyone compares tallies of cattle and brands sighted, we'll an have an idea

100

what's between here and Fort Ross."

"I've seen enough," said Hampton.

"These tin cases," Tom told them all, "hold powers of attorney I gathered in Texas. These tally books have brands and earmarks of stock run off by the Comanches. And the number of cattle and horses that different ranches have lost. Also dates of loss, and other sworn information. I'm not a lawyer, but in Texas I spoke with lawyers. I'm told that the right to recover these brands will stand in Texas or Territorial courts."

Ashley Hampton was rolling a smoke. His silent nod approved.

"But any man," Tom said, "who tries to replevin stolen stock in this Territory will find politics and hostility. Law will tie him up hopelessly. There's only one quick, certain way — take the stolen cattle where found on free range, and let so-called owners try to prove legal purchase from the rightful owners."

"Might I see one of those tally books?" Hampton inquired.

Tom handed him one. An ember popped in the small fire as Hampton scanned the pages of the tally book. "Many of these brands I know. And the losses in cattle and blood their owners have suffered." He looked up at Tom. "What do we get out of it?"

"What I offered men in Texas: half of all you help recover. Settle with the Texas owners yourselves. Men in Texas who can't come will accept a third of anything recovered, remitted when possible."

"Lucky to get it," Hampton murmured.

"Do you know of any other men on the way from Texas?"

"No, suh."

"We're not many," Tom said. "When we take the first cattle, men will rise against us. They'll know that if they stop us, they'll be able to stop other tries at their illegal stock. This is the time to wait for more help, or back out. If we start, we can't stop."

Ashley Hampton handed back the leather-bound book. "Might be a good idea to tally up now and see what the country holds."

The men drew small tally books from their pockets and began to call off brands of cattle and horses they had sighted in the wide sweep north. Tom checked against the brands he had brought from Texas, giving attention to ear-marks.

Now and then a man would exclaim, "I know that'n!" Other remarks burst out: "Him an' his oldest boy was kilt!" "Them folks got burnt out!" "I rode to their place nex' day. They was a bloody mess, womenfolks still acryin'." Once — quietly, fiercely — a Texan exclaimed, "*Them cattle is mine! They got my cousin, damn 'em!* Most twenty Comanch's jumped the place!"

Ashley Hampton spoke for them, soberly. "We will ride with you." He looked around at the other Texans, was satisfied, and drawled, "All the way."

They camped in the canyon that night, and rode at dawn, each man leading an extra horse he had brought. And as they emerged from the mouth of the canyon, the new sun burst up in the East. Southwest, the distant Secundos lifted under their placid white cloud caps.

Hampton, riding beside Tom, looked long and silently. Finally he spoke in a somber drawl, "Too fair a land to fatten on the blood of Texas."

And the next day, before noon, the sudden screaming of a bullet made Tom duck in the saddle. The hidden gun was to his right, in brush along the crest of this long, broken slope, which dropped into a wide, grassy draw.

Tom had just turned three lanky steers down the slope toward a small bunch of cattle which one of the Texans was holding. The steers bolted as the slapping gun report echoed. Tom slashed his horse with the rein ends, and raked his spurs. He saw the Texan grabbing for the carbine under his leg.

Tom put his plunging horse straight across the broken slope. Another bullet whipped by his neck. Too close! Only this spurred, furious race across the open slope held any safety. The Texan was riding full gallop down the draw.

Now they were hunted men!

Tom rode for a rain-gouged gully in the slope ahead. He put his horse recklessly over the gully bank, plunging down over eroded, yielding earth into the rough gully bottom. He spurred and slashed up the steep gully over rocks and wind-blown tumbleweeds. And he wondered how many guns were waiting in the brush above.

TEN

Carbine in hand, leaning low in the saddle, Tom rode a furious weaving charge through green junipers and branched cholla cactus along the crest of the wide, grassy draw. And in the brush ahead an indistinct figure moved convulsively on the ground. Tom reined in hard and tossed the reins to the ground as he jumped off.

He landed running, whipping up the carbine to shoot; and a shrill, warning whistle froze his finger on the trigger. Eagan's red face came up from the ground, yelling, "Don't shoot, Lieut'n't!"

Eagan was glowering at a stranger in leather chaps and brown vest who sprawled face down on the ground, arms stretched out. A carbine and revolver had been kicked away. Empty brass shells marked where the man had been shooting down into the draw.

"Eagan," Tom said, breathing hard, "you pop up in the damnedest places. You're supposed to be miles away."

"I was scoutin' around. When this fellow started shootin', he forgot to look back."

"You were riding flank on me, ready for trouble," Tom said. He ordered the stranger, "Sit up!"

The man pushed himself up and scowled malevolently. Eagan regarded him with hostility. "He grabbed for his holster. I had to bust him with my gun barrel."

The stranger wiped blood off his mouth with the back of his hand. The Texan's horse burst through the brush to them.

Tom called, "His horse is over there, tied to a juniper. Have a look at it." And to the prisoner, "What's your story?"

The man mumbled, "I ride for Ben Poole. Orders is to shoot rustlers."

"How many men ride for Poole?"

"Three."

The Texan shouted, "He's riding Cross D brand, vented!"

"Stand up," Tom said to the prisoner. On the short side, the man stood warily. Tom studied him. "This Ben Poole lives in that canyon some miles east of here, doesn't he?"

"Uh-huh."

"Get going! Walking!"

The man caught up his black hat and started. He looked back once, apprehensively. His steps lengthened out along the crest of the draw and he vanished in the brush. The lanky Texan rode back, leading a saddled horse.

"Take that horse," Tom said, "and shove the gather we made on to the main bunch. Tell

Ashley Hampton that Eagan and I are taking the man's guns and saddle to his boss."

"Ain't that askin' to get shot?" the Texan drawled.

"We'll risk it."

The Texan shrugged, and moments later departed with the horse. Eagan balanced the extra saddle and bridle before him on his horse. Tom took the man's carbine and revolver. They rode east, quartering knife ridges and gashed arroyos. Eagan had fallen into a morose mood.

Finally Eagan said, "All this don't look like you mean to go back in the Army."

"Did I ever say I would?"

"I figured you would."

"Why don't you pull out now for Fort Ross and enlist again?" Tom suggested.

Eagan considered it. "I'll stay around for the trouble," he muttered finally.

Tom's faint smile was understanding. Army had been home and family. Eagan was lonely for the reassuring routine, reveille to taps, and all the hours between fenced in with orders and custom. There were no bold, beckoning dreams in Eagan. But Eagan would stay. He was stubborn.

Miles to the east, they struck the wide, shallow canyon and rode along the brink of the immense trough. Glistening water in the canyon bottom wandered through white sands and gravels of the flood channel. Willows and chamiso thickets grew along the water.

"Good winter shelter down there," Tom commented.

Eagan was looking ahead, where two corrals were taking shape in the sun-flooded canyon. The ranch house, still invisible, would be among the tall cottonwoods which lifted between the corrals and the small stream. "This is risky," said Eagan dubiously.

"All of this is risky," Tom reminded him. "If we ever run from them, we'll never have a chance. I want to see if this Ben Poole bought his cattle and horses from Fallon."

Eagan kept silent as they followed the steep pitch of a crude wagon trail down the side of the canyon. The wheel ruts led them through bunch grass and low yucca clumps to the corrals. "Cheap-jack outfit!" Eagan said with distaste.

"Trying for a quick profit with cheap Comanche-raided cattle," Tom guessed, looking about.

The two sagging corrals, holding seven horses, had been carelessly constructed of cedar and juniper stobs thrust into trenches, dirt tramped around the bottoms, green cowhide strips sloppily woven among the tops. Three openfront sheds were as carelessly built of unplastered adobe bricks.

A long, low adobe shack squatted under the first towering cottonwoods. The back door was a soiled bullhide, nailed at the top. Tin cans and trash had been tossed out and left scattered on the ground. The man who shouldered out past the bullhide was solid and untidy.

"Howdy?" Tom called and got no reply. The flat cheeks and broad nose of the staring man were lined with purple veins. Under his dark mustache he slowly munched tobacco as Tom rode to him.

"I'm looking for Ben Poole," Tom said.

"You got him."

"I'm Cantrell, from the Frio country."

Poole spat a thin jet to one side. "Heerd of you," he said with more interest. "Startin' a big ranch, ain't you?" He eyed the saddle balanced in front of Eagan. "Lost a hoss?"

Tom placed his hands on the saddle horn, by the extra carbine hanging there from a leather thong. "The saddle belongs to one of your men. Give it to him, Eagan."

Poole looked surprised as he swung the saddle to the ground. "What happened?"

"Your man was riding a vented Cross D horse, Mr. Poole. Where did you get the horse?"

Poole's flat thumb hooked under a fraying suspender strap. "That's my business! What's it to you?"

"You're aware, I suppose, that the horse's owner was John Kent, in Texas."

"Mebbe."

"Kent never sold any horses. He lost stock twice in Comanche raids."

"That ain't my business."

"It's my business, Mr. Poole. I hold Kent's

power of attorney to recover any stock he's lost. You have your saddle and bridle; these guns belong to your man. He's walking in. I've taken the horse."

Poole's mouth had loosened under the tobacco-stained mustache. His temper flared. "What the hell is this? Comin' on a man's land, snatchin' his hoss!"

"You're using open range," Tom reminded him.

"My brand's on that hoss!"

"Where's your bill of sale from John Kent, in Texas?"

"Damn the bill of sale! I ain't no hoss thief!"

"A horse thief," Tom said coolly, "risks a bullet. You let Indians steal for you. Going to tell where you bought that horse?"

Poole's callused thumb had clamped hard on his suspender strap. His eyes were hating. "I ain't tellin' nothing. I'm through talkin'!"

Tom gave him a dark look. "I'm not through. Take your man's guns!" Poole came forward and caught the carbine and revolver Tom handed down. Tom ran the reins through his hand and gave the man another dark look. "Poole, you were jobbed by the man who sold you horses and cattle."

"Nev' mind."

"It's your worry. I'm taking about two hundred head of your cattle, too. They were raided out of Texas."

"Tryin' to take my cattle too?" burst from

110

Poole. It had a strangled sound.

"I've taken them," Tom said coldly. "After this, be careful what you buy."

Half-sobbing his rage, Poole jumped back. "No slicker with a long rope runs a whizzer on me!" His thick yell lifted: "*Stop 'em, boys! Only two here!*" Poole was jacking the carbine action and jerking the muzzle up.

Tom spun his horse as Poole pulled the trigger. The carbine did not fire. The plunging horse smashed into carbine and man.

Poole was slammed into the bullhide, and helplessly past it into the interior. The spin of Tom's horse brushed the doorway. His left stirrup struck the rotten adobe bricks beside the door frame and dragged off loose bits as the horse lunged along the house wall. As Tom reined around the end of the long shack, his quick look noted no window at this end, where guns could reach after them from shelter.

Eagan was close behind as they raced into dappled shade under the great cottonwoods, ducking low branches. The spiteful report of a carbine reached after them. More guns opened up. A storm-toppled cottonwood loomed across Tom's path. Massed roots bulked at one end; the tangle of dead branches started a few feet away. Tom rode at the short space of clear trunk. He yelled and lifted his horse over.

Eagan's hoarse yell was audible behind. The booming strike of a hoof on the tree made Tom look back. Eagan's horse was coming down in a half-stumble on the sandy soil. Eagan hauled its head up and the horse recovered stride.

The tangle of dead cottonwood top was a screen of sorts behind them as they raced out of the trees into glaring sunlight. Half a mile down the canyon, Tom pulled up and looked back. He was regretful when Eagan halted by him. "I hate to run horses like this."

Eagan's broad face was a deep, sweating red. "Them horses in the corrals were sure sign more men were in the house," Eagan said. "We almost got kilt there."

Tom grinned. "The other end of the house had no window, Eagan. Ben Poole was blocking the doorway. I had an idea that when he heard about his cattle, he'd not stop to see whether the shells had been taken out of the guns I handed him."

"We could have throwed revolvers on him when the talking started," Eagan grumbled.

"And had the men inside slipping around the ends of the house, boxing us," Tom said dryly. "I had my talk with Poole. Let's get out of this canyon."

They found a difficult way up the eroded steeps of the canyon and, from the rim, looked back. Horses had hurriedly been saddled at Poole's place. Men were riding out of the canyon on the opposite side.

"After help," Eagan guessed. "They'll have the country boilin'!"

"We expected it," Tom reminded him. "It will

be days before enough men get together to trouble us."

"And then what?" Eagan said under his breath.

Tom watched the distant riders climbing the opposite side of the canyon. Some of the deep, persisting smolder returned to his face. He said slowly, "Then you'll wish you were back in the Army, Eagan. And every man who owns stolen Texas stock will begin to know I'm in the Frio country to stay!"

ELEVEN

Virginia Bratton was sewing buttons on a blouse when Barnaby Polk came to the open door of her bedroom. Virginia looked up from her rocking chair, smiling at his tall, shirtsleeved figure with jaunty red suspenders across the lanky shoulders.

"Visitors are approaching," the Judge said.

"Is it Lee?" Virginia asked quickly.

"A young lady is coming, escorted by three soldiers," said the Judge. His glance grew quizzical. "Still worrying about Lee?"

"How can I help it?" Virginia dropped the blouse and thimble into the sewing basket beside her chair. She stood up, voicing the small fear which never quite left her these days: "Suppose Lee meets Cantrell and his men?"

"Lee went to Las Vegas, to buy cattle," the Judge said.

"And where is Tom Cantrell? He's been gone over a week now, with all those armed men!"

"Why not let Cantrell manage his half of the ranch as he pleases?" suggested the Judge dryly. "You ordered him to, emphatically. Remember?"

With shrewd logic, the Judge usually could

deflate her, Virginia thought ruefully as she walked outside, in front of the house. With pleasure she saw that a corporal and two troopers from Fort Ross were escorting Isabel Alcorn, the Major's daughter. She had met Isabel at the fort, and called a warm greeting. Isabel's reply was gay.

A trooper swung off and held Isabel's horse. The corporal jumped to give Isabel a hand down. Tall, smiling, Isabel stripped off her leather riding gloves and surveyed the massive adobe house. Her hat was white felt, her jacket soft doeskin; she was booted, with a riding crop tucked under her arm.

"The house is larger than I thought," Isabel said, approving. "Where is Tom Cantrell?"

"Gone over a week now, with his men," Virginia said, and she saw disappointment appear visibly on Isabel's face.

"Where did Tom go?"

"He didn't say," Virginia said. "Tea water is hot. And if you haven't eaten —"

"Tea will be nice," Isabel said politely.

Barnaby Polk was in the long living room, wearing his dignified black coat now. His blue, shrewd eyes twinkled at Isabel. "An old man hardly deserves two such delightful young ladies all to himself," said the Judge gallantly. "You will be with us some time, I hope, Miss Alcorn?"

"Only until tomorrow," Isabel said. She was thoroughly curious as she glanced about the big room.

Doña Sarina, plump and beaming in a gaudily flowered apron, brought tea and little spiced cookies called *biscochitos,* on a tray covered with bright hand-hammered tin. The Judge glanced at the teacups with a droll lack of enthusiasm. He murmured an excuse and unfolded from his chair.

Isabel's thoughtful glance followed his tall, gray-haired figure through the patio doorway. "Does Mr. Polk live here too?"

"I wish he did," Virginia said, pouring tea. "His old friend, Judge Augustus Andrews, is holding court in Mesilla, and will join him here for a few days, before they go to Santa Fe together." She handed a cup and saucer to Isabel and urged, "Can't you stay longer?"

Isabel shook her head. "I'll use Tom's room tonight, and start back to the fort in the morning."

Remembering Cantrell's spartan room she had viewed through his open doorway, Virginia said without thinking, "His bunk is hard and uncomfortable. I have a feather mattress."

Isabel's quick glance probed such intimate knowledge of Tom Cantrell's room. "Tom's bunk will do," she said coolly.

You should see how the man acts! Virginia thought angrily. And during the afternoon, with mixed feelings, she watched Isabel Alcorn calmly and coolly assume command of Cantrell's part of the house.

The Judge's dry tones penetrated Virginia's

116

thoughts. "For the third time, Ginny, the sunset is colorful!"

"Isn't it?" said Virginia, hastily. She looked west at the blaze of crimson above the bold Lizard Butte. "I was thinking what it would be like if Cantrell brought her here as his wife," Virginia confessed.

"The possibility," said the Judge, "had not occurred to me." His "Hm-m-m!" had a judicial sound. "Two women in the same house. Each owning half," the Judge mused. Reflective humor grew in his eyes.

"Isabel Alcorn," said Virginia, frowning, "is very nice, I'm sure. But it's plain already she'll always have her own way."

"A court of law," said the Judge gravely, "would have difficulty with such a case. There was a man named Solomon —" The Judge cleared his throat. "For my client, Ginny, I would plead, *exitus acta probat,* the outcome justifies the deeds."

"It is not amusing!" Virginia said. "This is my home. Everything I have is here now. You don't understand."

"An unregenerate old sinner," said the Judge, "could muse upon the possibilities. Especially upon our friend Cantrell, caught in the cross-fire."

"The man is a business partner, not a friend!"

"An unfortunate figure of speech," said the Judge. His veined hand dropped to her shoulder. "Ginny," he said quietly, "old sinners were young once. They do understand, even if they seem calloused."

"You were never calloused, and never a sinner, old or young," said Virginia. She covered his gnarled hand with her hand.

"Some of that could be debated," said the Judge. "However, Ginny, I want you to be happy in this home I advised you to buy. Suppose, before worrying, we wait for the worst to happen?"

"In other words, be sensible," Virginia said. She remembered Cantrell's warning: *Dead man's shoes on her feet!* She hadn't been afraid. Now, smiling, she looked up and nodded. The Judge's twinkling blue eyes looked back with approval.

And the next morning, with detached composure, Virginia was able to watch Isabel Alcorn impatiently lingering for some sign of Tom Cantrell's return. Finally, in the long living room, Isabel held out a brown sealed envelope.

"Will you give this to Tom when he returns?"

"Of course." Virginia took the envelope, thinking of the letter this disappointed girl must have penned in Cantrell's silent room last night.

"It is a copy of an Army report, with information about the death of Tom's former partner," Isabel said.

"Oh!" Suddenly the brown envelope was important. Virginia moistened her lips, remembering her flashes of uneasiness that Lee might be a target for the same guns which had murdered Steven Rogers. *Dead man's shoes on her feet! On Lee's feet too!* She asked, "Does the Army know who killed Rogers?"

"The Army isn't interested," Isabel said, drawing on her riding gloves. "But this report may give Tom some ideas." Isabel tapped the riding crop on her long skirt. "This place is not safe. Certainly not for you. And Tom, I believe, is in danger. He'll come back into the Army, eventually, of course. It's in his blood. He doesn't —" Isabel's glance ran over Virginia. "Tom doesn't belong with cattle."

"I wouldn't know," Virginia said, evenly, and she thought, *Do you really know him? I wonder.*

She stood silently out back with the Judge, watching Isabel and her escort canter off. She knew now Isabel's reluctance to leave another woman in this house to greet Cantrell's return. Isabel so obviously disapproved of the way Cantrell was forced to share his home.

Barnaby Polk gazed placidly after the riders. "She will be at Fort Ross," the Judge mused. "You will be here. *Facta non verba!*"

"What is that?" Virginia asked absently.

"Deeds, not words," said the Judge, reflectively.

During an afternoon after Lee Bratton had departed from the Gallinas ranch with a tough new crew, to meet and select his herd, Matthew Fallon indulged in some hours of complacent drinking.

It was a thing he seldom allowed himself to do. Whiskey stripped away intelligence and bared weaknesses to the world. He gave brusque orders first to the three men left on the ranch. He was not to be disturbed until the next morning. Then he locked the front and back doors of the stone house.

Sitting alone in the quiet parlor, in his undershirt, Fallon sipped whiskey from a water glass. Now and then he lighted a fresh cigar. His complacency grew. Heady satisfaction mounted when he thought of Lee Bratton's arrival at Cantrell's ranch, backed with that hard, armed crew.

Late in the afternoon, Fallon lifted the twisted claw of a hand from his lap and regarded it solemnly. His sudden giggle came from whiskey, he knew, and did not mind. He wanted to feel like this.

There was nothing, he knew disdainfully, that Matthew Fallon could not do with cool planning. Even Cantrell, in the distant Frio country, was not really a threat. Merely a bumbling young ex-cavalry officer, recklessly bent on being a cowman in the wildest part of the Territory. After Cantrell was swept aside, Matthew Fallon would stand astride all this vast, wild country, without opposition. Fallon lighted a fresh cigar and fell to musing about the small boy who had run away from the Apaches.

The roan horse that Cantrell had claimed, had come from a sub-chief named Senya, who had been hunting the boy. The Apache had produced the roan readily, asking only that Fallon and his men watch for the boy, and return him if possible.

Finding and returning the boy to the Apaches would have been an immense stroke of luck. Senya, with every fighting buck under him, would have been in Matthew Fallon's debt. Senya had been filled with shame that his adopted son, cherished proudly, had run away.

Fallon reached to the table at his elbow and filled the glass again, slopping whiskey over the side. Indians were simple savages. They risked their useless lives raiding cattle and horses, and then traded the loot for trinkets! They murdered and tortured like the heartless brutes they were. Then, childlike, they adopted a white boy and heaped great heart and pride on him. An intelligent man could use them as he wished. If the boy had been found and returned, Senya and his bucks would be available now to use against Cantrell. And no one in the Territory would suspect Matthew Fallon's part in a bloody Apache raid on Cantrell's ranch.

Fallon giggled again at the thought and gulped from the glass. His spasm of coughing spilled whiskey over his undershirt. The claw of a right hand absently rubbed the wet cloth as Fallon sat musing on how he would handle the Bratton girl and her brother after Cantrell was out of the way. When he reached again for the whiskey bottle, he realized groggily that the room was dark.

He got to his feet with an effort, and staggered and fell to the floor, losing the glass. Some small intelligent part of his brain mocked that he was gutter drunk. A gentleman got to his bed, if possible. Carefully, slowly, with tremendous concentration, Fallon stood up.

Holding to the glimmer of reason, he groped and staggered across the dark room, and into his bedroom. When he came against the edge of the iron bed, he fell heavily on it, face down, satisfied.

In the morning, a fist, hammering on the back door, made him painfully open his eyes. The first gray cheerless dawn hung outside the bedroom window. The urgent hammering on the back door continued. Matthew Fallon's name was loudly called. Mumbling, Fallon stiffly got off the bed. He groaned with the first lurching step. Pain stabbed his skull. A foul taste was in his mouth. His nerves were raw as he made his way to the locked back door and demanded, "What's wrong?"

The voice outside was furious. "I'm Ben Poole! Rode since yesterday to get here! A damned thief named Cantrell, from the Frio country, run off my cattle! Said they was stole in Texas an' ain't mine! You sold 'em, Fallon! What about it?"

"Wait until I get dressed."

Swearing under his breath, Fallon walked unsteadily into the parlor. The bottle beside the table lamp still held some whiskey. He drank

122

from the bottle. It helped a little. He'd slept in shoes and pants; but he never appeared before other men without a coat pocket where his right hand could stay, out of sight. Fully awake, nerves jumpy, Fallon stepped into the bedroom and pulled on a shirt and coat.

The dawn was brighter when he emerged from the back door, his hand in the coat pocket. Ben Poole's solid, untidy figure stood by a sagging, half-dead horse. Poole was vehemently talking to the three men from the bunkhouse. In sullen rage at the thought of Cantrell, Fallon walked to the group.

"What happened?" he brusquely asked Ben Poole.

Purple veins on Poole's flat cheeks and large nose looked swollen. He was a furious, almost incoherent man despite the punishing ride he had made. Presently Fallon cut rudely into the torrent of words.

"Three other men in your house? And Cantrell rode up with only one man? And told you he was taking cattle and horses from you, and rode away safely?"

"The damn gun wouldn't fire! Mighta been twenty more men waiting out of sight!" Poole said resentfully.

"You don't even know how many men Cantrell had!" Fallon said disgustedly.

"He had enough to feel damn certain of hisself! An' you ain't out of it, Fallon! He knowed who them cattle belonged to in Texas!

123

Kept trying to find out where I bought 'em!"

"Did you tell him?"

"Told him nothin'. But if he keeps pickin' up Texas cattle, he'll gut a strip of the range from my place to the Frio. Ain't there no way to get the law on him?"

"What law?" Fallon asked in surly scorn.

Ben Poole's heavy cheek muscles were bunching under dark stubble as he chewed tobacco hard. He spat forcibly. "Small folks like me ain't got the men to fight when we're stole out of pocket. We bought from you. Do we get help?"

Raw resentment jumped with the pain in Fallon's head. He hated this flat-faced Ben Poole for the dawn commotion Poole had made. And hated Cantrell worse. Cantrell was on the loose now, undoubtedly making a sweep back to his ranch. South toward the Frio country from Poole's place, Cantrell would probably cross Largo Canyon, where some of Fallon's own cattle were held.

"Cantrell lost his Texas herd, so he's stealing from honest men," Fallon managed to say coolly. "If he gets by with this, he'll be back again. Nothing to do but smash him quick. Drive him back to his new ranch, and run him off his ranch and out of the country."

"It'll be a sweet day!" Ben Poole growled.

"Cantrell only had four men and himself the other day," Fallon recalled.

"*Four?*" Poole repeated, unbelievingly.

"He may have picked up another man or two. I have three men at Largo Canyon. We might head him off there. We'll scatter out," Fallon decided, "and gather up help on the way to Largo Canyon. Where are your men?"

"Went for help."

"Go back by your place and see what help is there. We'll eat and get ready."

One of Fallon's men said, "What about the crew that went with young Bratton?"

"They'll be busy."

He had been thinking about Lee Bratton. As he walked back to the house, Fallon decided to let that affair stand. It was plain now what would happen if young Bratton got back to the ranch with the cattle he had bought, and Cantrell managed to get safely back to the ranch. Fallon even managed to find a thin smile. One way or another, Cantrell's time was running fast out.

TWELVE

The deep-toned report of the sunset gun had rolled majestically across the earth-built structures that were Fort Ross. The high, streaming flag had been run down from the white pole on the sun-baked parade ground. Guard mount and bugle-laced retreat had ended the orderly activities of another day when Isabel Alcorn and her escort returned from Tom Cantrell's ranch.

Major Alcorn had paused at the front door of his quarters to wipe the sweatband of his gilt-corded black hat. His final, critical glance about the quadrangle sighted Isabel on her sidesaddle. With warming anticipation, Alcorn walked slowly out to the hitchrack and watched Isabel, followed by the corporal, put her horse into a final canter across the deserted parade.

As he waited, Alcorn smiled fondly and wryly. Isabel had been so certain that she had maneuvered a slightly reluctant father into permission to visit Cantrell's ranch. Alcorn was fully aware, indulgently at times, irritably at other times, of Isabel's talent for having her own way.

In this matter, Isabel's insistence had been a

help. She had known nothing of Tom Cantrell's scheme of taking Texas cattle by force. Her visit to Cantrell's ranch would undoubtedly draw out the latest details now of Cantrell's intentions. There was even a small chance Isabel might yet toll Cantrell back into the regiment.

Isabel reached him and tossed her reins to the corporal. Alcorn gave her a hand down and dismissed the corporal. Smiling, he said, "You didn't stay long."

Isabel looked tired as she removed her white felt hat. "Tom wasn't there," she said, not hiding her disappointment.

The corporal had ridden out of earshot, leading Isabel's horse. Casually Alcorn inquired, "Where is Cantrell?"

"That girl at the ranch, Miss Bratton, didn't know." Isabel was removing her gloves with impatient jerks. "Tom has been gone over a week."

"I see," Alcorn said, thoughtfully. "Take anyone with him?"

"That boy who ran away from the Apaches was there," Isabel said. "He told the corporal that Tom had taken all his men, and left with six strange Texans who had arrived at the ranch the day before."

"Tom needs cattle," Alcorn said non-committally.

"I suppose so." Forgetting her disappointment, Isabel said, "The boy asked the corporal if Tom had gone to get his mother. He wanted to know if the soldiers were going to help. Dad, can't something be done for that woman?"

"I'm sorry," Alcorn said regretfully. "Not at this time."

"I keep thinking of her."

"It can't help the woman, or you," Alcorn said, and changed the subject. "You'll find Tom next time," he suggested, smiling. "Get some rest before dinner. I'll be in shortly."

He had been anticipating dinner. Now, when the house door closed behind Isabel, Alcorn lighted a cigar and walked slowly along the row, thinking.

The smell of heat and dust from the hot day blended with the fragrance of piñon and cedar smoke from kitchen ranges. The blue-gray of first twilight was moving in, overshot by the brighter blue of the upper sky, where the vanished sun still reached. At the end of the row where Alcorn waited, slowly chewing his cigar, he presently sighted the man he wanted coming from the stables.

"Mr. Fitzpatrick!" Alcorn called.

"Yes, sir!"

In blues and gilt buttons, black kerchief at his neck, Second Lieutenant Fitzpatrick reminded Alcorn of Tom Cantrell, at Cantrell's best. "Walk out on the parade with me," Alcorn said pleasantly.

"Pleasure, sir!"

They strolled out on the deserted parade. Fitzpatrick, obviously, was curious. Undoubtedly he was canvassing his shortcomings, wondering what the Old Man was up to. Alcorn took the cigar from his mouth. "You and Tom Cantrell were close friends at Fort Union, I remember."

"We were, Major."

"You'll not relish the orders I'm placing you under now," Alcorn said without emotion. "You'll not discuss them with anyone." Alcorn inspected the frayed end of his cigar. "I'll have to explain. Tom Cantrell lost his Texas herd and needs cattle. He has a reckless scheme to take forcibly livestock that have allegedly been stolen in Texas by the Comanches."

Fitzpatrick's soft whistle was followed by a faint grin of admiration. "Wouldn't Tom Cantrell come up with something like that!"

"He would!" Alcorn made it stinging. Fitzpatrick reddened and silently waited.

"To make it worse," Alcorn said, calmly again, "Cantrell arranged to have Texans join him. I have reason to believe he's out now, with his ranch crew and a party of Texans. You can guess what will happen."

Fitzpatrick's comment was a cautious understatement. "Tom won't find much of a welcome."

"Texas gunmen loose in the Territory, taking livestock forcibly, will mean shooting and killing," Alcorn said tersely. "Much of it will draw in Apaches, Comanches, and perhaps even Kiowas."

"Does Tom have any sort of legal basis for such actions?" Fitzpatrick inquired carefully.

"Legality," said Alcorn brusquely, "is for courts and lawyers. There is no law in this district. Fort Ross has orders to pacify and protect. In the morning you take out a patrol and discover what may be happening."

"Shall I patrol to Cantrell's ranch, Major?"

"Tom Cantrell won't be taking cattle off his own ranch," Alcorn said caustically. "Scout to roughly a hundred miles north of his ranch. You might cover the upper Frio Plaza for any loose talk about Cantrell's intentions. Separate your men as you please. Ostensibly, and actually also, you will be looking for hostile Apaches and Comanches."

Cool now, Fitzpatrick inquired, "If I run into trouble involving Tom Cantrell, shall I take a hand?"

"Don't even go near Cantrell. Inform me by courier of any trouble involving Cantrell."

"Yes, sir."

The hoarse bawling of the advancing cattle was continuous. The scuffing hoofs struck the dry earth into fine dust which lifted and swirled, settled and clung. Tom Cantrell could taste the dust as he rode to the point of the growing herd.

Ashley Hampton, the rangy Texan, was riding watchfully out ahead of the herd. He smiled as Tom pulled the dusty kerchief off his face.

"Justice," the Texan said, "plagues this land

and the inhabitants thereof!" He pointed to the east where a small bunch of cattle was breaking over a brush-studded rise, hazed along by three riders with carbines ready across their thighs. A sternness came on the Texan's tired, unshaven face. "Every hoof," he added with a bite, "stole in Texas, in tears and blood!"

"And we'll see more blood when enough men get together behind us," Tom said soberly.

The Texan nodded. Tom rode thinking of threats which had been hurled at them, and flurries of gunfire, usually at a distance, as they made this fast sweep south toward the Frio country.

The men were ranging out for miles, sweeping cattle and horses back to the growing herd. Like General Sherman's foraging bummers gutting a strip through Georgia, Ashley Hampton had commented grimly. Only this was more pleasure to think about.

West, the dark canyons and sheer escarpments of the Secundos were bold against the blue sky. Ashley Hampton gauged them and scanned the country ahead. "We're 'most to that big canyon-like valley I was tellin' you about."

"It must be Largo Canyon," Tom guessed. "Water in it, you said?"

"And cattle for us," the Texan said grimly. "We can move down the canyon, gather the cattle, an' bed along the water."

"Not in a canyon. We'd be targets from the rim. I'll take men and push the cattle in the canyon up to where we're crossing," Tom decided. "We'll bed to the south tonight." He was watching one of the three approaching riders running his horse out ahead to join them. "That's George Sell. Something's happened," Tom said.

George Sell had shoved his carbine into the saddle scabbard. The same tired, fierce look furrowed George's face behind his brown mustaches when he neared them. They had all been riding from dawn until dark, with only brief snatches of sleep at night.

George spoke tersely as he pulled his horse to a walk beside them. "Three men won't be enough out that way again! We run into five strangers who had an idea they'd cut us off."

"They didn't, looks like," Ashley Hampton drawled.

"Hot for a time," George said. "Buck Ellis took a bullet through his hat. We run 'em two-three miles. Hit one in the arm. It discouraged 'em. But they'll be back with more." George wiped his face with the end of his blue kerchief. "That ain't all. I saw a trooper watching the fun from a ridge over east of us."

Tom asked sharply, "Are you certain he was a trooper?"

"Wasn't half a mile away, plain against the sky, watchin' through glasses."

"Just one?"

"All we seen."

"One trooper means more," Tom said.

"Could be a routine patrol that heard the shooting." He had not told these men of Major Alcorn's threat to intervene, and did not now. "I'll take three men ahead, and come back up the canyon," Tom decided. "With luck, we'll find you watering in the canyon. Hold the rest of the men in close."

Tom chose Eagan, Pete Yancey, and one of Hampton's Texans. They cut off southeast, saving their horses, riding watchfully. The furious gun battle inevitably shaping would not come today, Tom had decided. But beyond the horizons enraged men were gathering.

The canyon which gashed across the landscape opened suddenly before them, a half-mile wide, with walls of red and yellow rock, and cattle grazing in the bottom. Tom used his binoculars.

"Texas brands down there," he said after some study.

They followed the rim, looking for a way down. Beyond a wide bend, a clump of green cottonwoods lifted beside the glinting band of water threading the canyon floor.

Eagan shaded his eyes with a palm. "Ain't that a wagon by them trees?"

Tom used the glasses again. "Have a look, Eagan!"

The odd note in Tom's voice drew a questioning glance from Eagan as he reached for the binoculars. Amazement appeared on Eagan's red, bristle-covered face as he peered intently.

"Old Sam Butterworth, sittin' by the fire!" Eagan blurted.

"Sam," Tom said, "should be in a hospital cot at Port Ross! That wounded leg of his can't be well."

Eagan returned the glasses, shaking his head head wordlessly. Some distance on they found where the wagon had descended into the canyon. The rocky trail was difficult, even for horses. A barricade of brush at the bottom blocked the trail to cattle in the canyon.

Two saddle horses were staked out near the wagon. A blackened coffee pot rested on a smoldering fire. Two rough-looking men with carbines held ready waited silently by the fire as Tom rode up.

Sam Butterworth sat with his back against the rear wheel of the wagon, wearing the same old greasy leather shirt belted at the middle with rope. Sam's sparse, iron-gray beard and wrinkled features looked as irascible as ever as he gnawed meat off a strip of jerky. Sam's big buffalo Sharps lay on the ground beside him. Chewing slowly on the jerky, Sam ignored them.

The muzzles of two carbines covered them.

Tom studied the silent, challenging men a moment before saying, "I'm Tom Cantrell. Whose cattle are these?"

It brought quick, narrowing interest. "You the Cantrell who whipped Lee Bratton?" the taller one asked. He was a heavy man with a tangle of brown beard, and hair matting the backs of big hands which held the carbine.

"I'm the man."

"Out buyin' cattle?"

"I'm looking for cattle. These yours?"

"Might be."

"I'm taking them."

"*What's that?*"

"They were Comanche stolen in Texas." It was an old story now; Tom was brief. "I'm recovering them for their owners."

"Jake!" the man said, not taking his gaze off Tom. "Takin' 'em, he says!"

"You can try that with a gun," Tom said evenly, "or drop it! Make your choice."

Still chewing the jerky, Sam Butterworth picked up his long, heavy rifle. "He'll drop it," Sam said.

The two men froze, not risking a look back while four armed men faced them.

"Sam, do they own these cattle?" Tom inquired.

"Ain't said. They's one more man down the canyon."

The larger man swore in his tangled beard. "Jake, I told you we oughta run the old buzzard off! He sneaked in last night just for this!"

"It'd been an idea," Sam said. "You shoot now, an' I'll shoot."

The carbines thudded to the ground. Eagan and the others had their revolvers out an instant later.

Tom dismounted and walked to the wagon, grinning. "How's the leg, Sam?"

Sam had put his rifle on the ground. He gnawed off another bite of jerky. "Still got it," he said. "Wrop enough fer four legs. That major's gal come back from your ranch with word Texans was out with you. I knowed what that meant. The doc throwed a fit when I hired me a hoss and saddle from the sutler an' come on. I knowed you'd be out this way, some'eres. Wasn't much welcome here, but I laid up a day to rest."

"We'll push the cattle up the canyon a few miles, where our herd is crossing," Tom said. "Can you ride with us?"

"Tie these two up. I'll watch 'em while you clean the canyon," Sam said placidly. "Then watch me ride."

At the end of this same day, when purple shadows filled the canyon bottom, Matthew Fallon let his shock and rage rake the three men who faced him by the wagon fire. "Cantrell came into the canyon with only three men? And took all the cattle you were hired to watch?"

The surly retort from the man with the matted brown beard was no help to Fallon. "Cantrell an' his men was in front of us. That old buzzard was back of us with his rifle. What would you have done?"

"Used my head! Not let a stranger loaf around all night and day!" Fallon stood with his twisted right hand clenched in the coat pocket. "Did the old man have a Sharps rifle? And a scraggly beard?"

"That's him."

"Pour me coffee!"

Fallon moved away from the fire with the tin cup of coffee. He had been in a savage humor over Cantrell since Ben Poole had wakened him at dawn yesterday. Temper, Fallon knew, was not the answer. Cantrell was moving south fast to the Frio country. Fallon surveyed the eight men standing around the fire, glumly drinking coffee. He had met two of them this afternoon, discouraged from a brush with Cantrell's men. Thinking hard, Fallon moved back to the fire.

"In two or three days," he said with cool confidence, "we'll have enough men. Ben Poole is collecting them at his ranch. I've sent my men out to spread the word about Cantrell. On the way here, I started everyone I met riding for help."

They eyed him in glum silence, waiting obviously for him to think for them. He despised them, while he talked coolly, confidently to them.

"Cantrell watered his cattle and pushed out of the canyon late this afternoon. He can't be far away. If we can stampede his herd tonight, he'll be held up a day or two. By then men will be gathering here at the canyon to stop him."

Their interest was visibly sharpening. "No moon tonight," Fallon said. "Cantrell can't have many men. Some of them will be asleep. Once his herd stampedes, he's in trouble. Anyone have a better idea?" And when he heard none, Fallon decided, "We'll hit Cantrell tonight, then."

THIRTEEN

A hand touched Tom Cantrell's shoulder, and he was instantly awake catching for the holstered gun in the blanket.

"After midnight, Lieut'n't," Eagan's voice said.

Tom stood up, buckling on his gun belt and yawning. "Everything all right?"

"Quiet," said Eagan. "Like nights when we were patrolling in hostile country."

Tom yawned again. "Eagan, you're going to have to reenlist. I can see that."

"No hurry," Eagan muttered.

But it was working in Eagan, Tom thought regretfully as he tied his rolled blanket behind the saddle of his waiting horse. The Army was home and family to Eagan. The big sergeant was lonely and lost in civilian life.

In the wan starlight, sleeping figures lay on the ground, a saddled horse ready on a short picket by each man. Eagan was spreading his blanket on the earth as Tom led his horse away from the sleeping men and stepped stiffly into the saddle.

Small restless sounds came from the bedded

herd as Tom walked his horse through the starlight. Low hills half a mile east were visible. The Secundos towered black and indistinct in the west. Far westward the booming howl of a wolf floated to the stars, and a shadowy rider loomed ahead, holding a long rifle across his lap.

"Sam, you should be asleep, resting that leg," Tom said as they fell in together.

"Young fellers need the sleep," said Sam, placidly. "They ain't no good readin' the night anyway."

Tom chuckled. "You've been riding this country long enough to outguess it, Sam."

"Seen it forty year ago," Sam said. "Stretchin' out like it had fer a million years, no good to anyone."

"I've thought of it that way too," Tom admitted.

"Seen towns on it, an' cattle everywhere, didn't you?"

"Something like that," Tom said, smiling. "It made me turn in my commission, and get out to help put the towns and cattle here."

"Forty year ago," Sam mused, "Mexico owned it. But the Indians knowed who really bossed it. I seen it too soon. But I usta figure babies was bein' born who'd do something about it."

Tom had the queer feeling he was hearing a voice out of the past, regretting dreams which had been told and too soon. He listened intently to Sam's words.

140

"When you quit the Army, I seen it in you an' come along to help." Sam sounded slightly embarrassed. "Kinda like old Sam had growed six feet tall in you, boy. All young an' brash again, and a chance to get roots down. Maybe a pretty wife an' kids who'd want a man around when he got old."

Tom smiled in the dark. "I'm not interested in a pretty wife." He regarded the hunched, shadowy figure of this often vitriolic little man, who had seen so much and done so much. And who still held the hungers of youth. "Sam, you'll see it happen now. And you'll be wanted. There's a home for you on the ranch to the end, part of everything."

"You got a big heart," Sam said. In the starlight his hunched shoulders started to shake. "I knowed that'd get you soft as mush," Sam chortled. "Soft heart, soft head, Tom! You won't build nothin' in this country if you git soft!"

Tom had to grin ruefully. "I'm not soft, Sam. I'm mad, and I stay mad. They won't stop me now!"

"You ain't homesick for the Army?"

"No."

"That major's gal come to the fort hospital. She seemed to figure you was still Army inside."

"Isabel is wrong."

"A managin' gal," Sam said. After a moment he added, "That little black-haired partner you throwed in the wagon at me is kind of spunky. She shot at them 'Paches real cool."

141

"Stubborn!" Tom said shortly. "She'll cause trouble yet!"

"I heard about your fight with her brother. That one'll make the trouble."

"They're a pair," Tom said. He rode thinking of her small figure beside him, in front of the house they owned together. She had hardly reached to his shoulder. The starlight had glinted off her pink basque and exotic shawl, and made every curve of her small face deceptively soft. And she had not budged an inch!

They met one of the Texans riding his slow circle, exchanged brief words and walked their horses on. Sam Butterworth was silent, until he suddenly said, "Them coyotes in the ridges over east has shut up! Five minutes ago coyotes quit to the north!"

Tom halted his horse, testing the night. "Trouble, Sam?"

"They ain't sleepy."

Tom made an immediate decision. "Tell the wrangler to push the horse herd a mile or so south. I'll get the men in their saddles."

Minutes later Tom wakened the snoring Ashley Hampton. The Texan came instantly out of his blanket, bringing up one of his long-barreled revolvers. He lowered it when Tom spoke.

"Could be a false alarm," Tom said, of the coyotes. "But if not, we'd better be ready."

Hampton was already folding his blanket, laying it behind his saddle. "Time for our luck to

142

run out," he drawled. "I'd pick a night like this if I was them, and nigh eight hundred head bedded and ready to scatter."

"If the cattle run, try to hold them south," Tom urged.

He was reaching for his stirrup when Sam's big buffalo gun, out east of the bedded cattle, slammed through the quiet night. Ashley Hampton waked the other sleeping men with a wild rebel yell as Tom went fast into the saddle.

Other guns smashed the night north and east of the herd, the nearest some hundreds of yards away. Sam's keen senses had jumped the attack before it was ready, Tom guessed as his horse bolted into a run. Behind him Ashley Hampton was shouting, "Nev' mind blankets! Keep south! South!"

The last was barely audible as hundreds of snorting, alarmed cattle lunged up on the bed ground. If they broke in the wrong direction, not much could be done. North a few miles, a stampede could pour blindly over the canyon drop. East and west were broken ridges. This bed ground had been selected because the country opened south for miles.

Tom spurred to the north side of the bed ground, firing his revolver, shouting. Wild at best, the herd broke in panic toward the south, where there were no guns and shouting men. The aimless tumult changed into the deep, dreadful roll of a stampede gathering momentum. Thousands of heavy hoofs hammered the earth in unison, faster and faster. Dust began to swirl up as Tom reloaded his revolver on the run and veered east.

No time to wonder about Sam Butterworth or the horse herd. Barely audible gunfire on the west side of the running herd showed that Hampton had men in place there.

The cattle were running faster, massing closer. Revolver in hand, Tom spurred up the east flank of the bolting mass. Two riders were cutting in ahead of him, yelling, firing revolvers directly at the herd. The shadowy mass of a running steer stumbled, plunged down and rolled. Tom bore out toward the indistinct riders, throwing shots at them. One man veered away; the other followed, and they dropped back out of sight as the rumbling thunder of the stampede swept south.

It could be worse, Tom thought. An inky night, a storm with thunder, lightning and sheeting rain, could have scattered the cattle beyond recovery for days. No other strangers rode in from this side. After a time Tom began to worry about Sam Butterworth.

Two hours later the cattle were still running south, but more slowly, less wildly. They had dropped to an uneasy trot when the sky lighted faintly in the east. By full dawn the pace had dropped to a shuffling walk. All the men but Sam Butterworth were with the herd. Tom rode to the front, where Ashley Hampton and three men were riding with carbines across their thighs, closely watching all nearby cover. Some eighty horses they had gathered with the cattle were out ahead, still together.

The Texan drawled, "Wasn't so many jumped us, evidently."

"Enough, if Sam Butterworth hadn't been watching last night," Tom said. "We'll push straight for the ranch now. With luck we can get there tomorrow night, before enough men gather behind us to make a real fight."

"That's best, probably," Hampton agreed. He brushed at his yellow mustache. His eyes were red-rimmed. He was frosted with dust, like all of them. "We'll fight 'em better without a herd to watch. Your house will make a good fort."

"I was thinking of that too." Tom smiled faintly, then sobered again. "I'm going to take Eagan and look for Sam Butterworth."

"Your place is here, running this, Cantrell," Hampton said quickly. "Best let me go."

"Sam is one of my men," Tom said as he turned his horse back.

Eagan was concerned as they rode back along the churned path of the stampede. "Reckon old Sam got throwed and tramped?"

"Sam was in the clear when it started, I think," Tom recalled. "He may have been shot, or his horse downed."

"If they get their hands on Sam, he's a goner."

"So are we," Tom reminded him dryly. "Don't get careless."

It was Eagan, almost an hour later, who jerked up his carbine, then blurted, "Look at that!"

Sam Butterworth was riding out from behind scrub cedars not a hundred yards away. Long rifle balanced across his saddle, hat pulled low, Sam looked hunched, gnome-like in his old leather shirt as he walked his horse toward them and leisurely gnawed on a chunk of meat.

"You two lost?" Sam called.

"All this ride, and him loafing around, eatin'!" Eagan said acidly as Sam joined them.

"I ain't stampeding all night with a wropped leg," Sam said calmly. "I rode over in the nearest brush and come on easy. Shot me a rabbit at daylight an' cooked a bite, like any man with sense. Bet you ain't et."

"No time, hunting you!" Eagan wet his lips and enviously eyed the well-browned haunch of jackrabbit in Sam's gnarled hand.

Tom was smiling with relief. "We're pushing straight through to the ranch now, Sam."

"If you get there," said Sam. "After the dust died down, I heerd one of them yell for a man named Fallon. And get his answer."

"Fallon?" Tom said.

Sam nodded. He gnawed off a bite of meat, saw Eagan staring ravenously, and held the rabbit haunch out to Eagan. "Two bites!" Sam said. "Your droolin' takes a man's appetite."

Sam chewed his meat, swallowed it, and said to Tom, "Fallon yelled for the men to get back to the canyon. Told them there'd be enough help in a day or so to do the job right." Sam leaned over and took his rabbit meat firmly back from

Eagan's fist. Sam's blue splintery glance turned to Tom. "Fallon sounded like he was sure of enough men," he said, "You better get set, Tom, for a showdown fight."

FOURTEEN

The next morning they sighted the bold yellow mass of the Lizard Butte, and pointed the weary herd at it. The men were haggard, red-eyed. Two were wounded, not seriously. But not a man showed any wish to leave. Hampton and his Texans had proved themselves. Their fierce purpose was visible as they rode watching the distance behind, ready for the guns gathering behind them.

Near midday, through his binoculars, Tom saw the ranch house clearly. He returned the glasses to the leather case at his saddle pommel and spoke to Ashley Hampton, riding beside him. "We'll bed the herd in that big draw south of the house. The grass is good. There's enough water from springs at the foot of the butte, and the house will be close."

Hampton's teeth gleamed under the yellow mustache. "That house will make them think. It's a fort."

"We built for something like this, and Apache raids," Tom said. "May save the ranch now." He rode for some minutes, thinking of what was

148

ahead. "They could jump us tonight," he said. "I'm going to send Eagan to the top of the Lizard Butte with my binoculars. He can watch more country from up there than we can. Even an hour's warning will help. Eagan can take a mirror and flash a warning from the top of the butte if there's sun."

"Suppose they've taken over the house before we get there?" Hampton drawled.

Tom frowned at the possibility. "Fallon would be the man to think of it. I'll go with Eagan." He smiled wryly. "If I don't come back, you'll know we have guests."

Tom rode from the bawling herd with Eagan; and as they loped over familiar miles of his own land, Tom put the binoculars now and then on the house. When their horses trotted into the wide yard behind the house, and they dismounted at the corral, Tom stood a moment surveying the bunkhouse and out-buildings, and the house itself. Everything here gave him a renewed sense of accomplishment. Here the future would be solidly rooted, after it had been savagely fought for in the hours ahead.

Tom started to the house, and noticed the small, tanned figure of the boy moving uncertainly from the saddle shed toward the corral. Tom heard Eagan's gruff, offhand greeting to the boy: "Hiya, kid? Been doin' all right?"

If the boy replied, Tom did not hear him. Barnaby Polk, the tall old lawyer, had emerged

149

from the back door of the house. "Welcome home, young man."

Tom smiled. "Glad to see you still here, sir."

"It has been a pleasant visit," the old lawyer said. "Ending too soon, I fear."

"Are you leaving?" Tom asked courteously.

"Tomorrow or next day," said Barnaby Polk, "my old friend, Judge Augustus Andrews, should arrive from Mesilla, where he has been holding court. We will go to Santa Fe together." He regarded Tom's haggard, dusty figure. "A hard trip, evidently."

"Not easy. We're bedding a herd near the house tonight. I rode in for a talk with Miss Bratton. Is she here?"

"In her room, I believe. Sarina is in the kitchen, and will tell Ginny."

The old lawyer was curious, Tom sensed as he walked on into the house. A smell of fresh-baked bread filled the kitchen. Sarina, the buxom Mexican woman, enveloped in an apron of bright flower print, beamed at him. Her hand indicated a cup of black coffee and a plate of cookies on the kitchen table.

"For me?" Tom asked in surprise.

"*Si!*"

Tom grinned at her. "Like home. Will you tell Miss Bratton I'd like to speak with her?"

"I tell!" She hurried toward the front part of the house.

Tom could feel the long strain and bone-weariness relaxing as he picked up the coffee cup and two cookies. The home-like feeling of this kitchen was soothing after the grueling days and nights. It gave a brief false sense of peace, of security against the trouble ahead. He carried the coffee and cookies into the spacious patio in the center of the big house and looked around critically.

The well he and Steve had dug in the center of this patio would be needed if the house were besieged. The thick, high adobe walls of the patio would not easily be breached. He inspected every shutter and loophole, through which they'd probably soon be holding off furious men and guns.

The Mexican woman returned through the patio, smiling. "She come."

Moments later Virginia Bratton stepped into the warm sunshine which filled the front half of the patio. "You wanted me, Mr. Cantrell?"

Her voice was pleasant and neutral. Her fine black hair, rolled back and pinned high, caught the sunlight in tiny gleams. She looked even smaller, more slender, in the crisp white blouse and plain black skirt, and earrings of tiny, intricate Mexican silver wirework. A massive silver bracelet on her slender left wrist caught the sun as she advanced.

Still held by the sense of homelike peace, Tom smiled and indicated the cookies and coffee he held. "Nice to find this waiting after a hard ride."

"Sarina likes to please the men."

"She could do worse," said Tom amiably. He gestured with the coffee cup to the log well curbing. "A seat ma'am?" And as she sat down, Tom glanced again around the patio. "Someday I'll have chairs here, and roofed walks along the sides, and rooms built outside. Flowers, too; hollyhocks, all colors."

Virginia looked around the patio. "Roses on trellises would do well. Yellow and white and red roses."

"I like roses," Tom said absently. He was studying the way a silver earring lay against her slender neck as she sat on the well curbing, head bent slightly, eyes half-closed. She was smiling faintly as she visualized the walks and flowers. She looked up into his gaze, and sat motionless. Slowly her eyes opened wide; deep-blue eyes against fair skin and the blackest hair, Tom noted.

She was probably judging his haggard, unshaved face, his dirty trail clothes and sagging gun belt. The thought reminded him of the boiling trouble that was coming. And what had to be done.

"Right now," he said thoughtfully, "you'll have to move back to the Frio Plazas, I'm afraid. I rode in to tell you."

She closed her eyes. "You did say move, didn't you, Mr. Cantrell?"

"You should get out today," Tom said. "Going to be trouble here. The place won't be safe for women. Use my wagon, if you like."

"Move out today?" Her voice had a stricken sound. "You are suggesting that I move out of this house which is half mine? Out of my own home?"

"I'm telling you to move," Tom said. "We're bringing a herd in close to the house. There's going to be trouble."

She stood up. "A herd? You've done well, Mr. Cantrell, for a man who lost his cattle and my cattle, and said he had no money to buy more!" She drew a breath. "Could this be the Texas herd you claimed to have lost?"

"Now you're talking like your brother," Tom said, cooling. He drank the last of the coffee and placed the empty cup on top of the windlass post of the well. "I took this herd from men who had bought illegally from the Comanche traders."

"You *took* a herd?"

"Where we found them. Now we've got to fight to hold them. Anything may happen here." Tom regarded her unsmilingly. "I saw this coming, and didn't want a girl for a partner. Now I'll not have a dead woman on my conscience. I'll have to order you to move out before the trouble hits."

"*You* order *me?*"

"I'm trying to help you. Trying to be reasonable."

"When were you ever reasonable?" She was breathing faster as she took two steps to the right and turned back. "What right have you to put

153

this ranch in danger? This ranch and this house, which are half mine!"

"We can settle that later. Right now you'll have to get out."

"Oh, will I?" She moved away again, and turned back, flushed. "How could you bring danger and trouble on the home I'm trying to make for myself and my brother? Everything we have is here!"

"Your brother seems to be able to take care of himself," Tom said, unimpressed. "Today I'll have to take care of you."

"You were never more mistaken, Mr. Cantrell!"

Her agitated steps were moving away again. Tom followed her, remembering old Sam Butterworth's tart advice, *Soft heart, soft head!* "Will I have to put you in the wagon, Miss Bratton?"

She whirled back. "Again in that wagon? *Never*, Mr. Cantrell! You humiliated me once!" She pushed the heavy silver bracelet up her arm and pulled it down. Her agitated steps went past him, and came back. "What kind of a woman do you think I am? To be bullied simply because you've stolen cattle!"

"I took them on open range!" Tom said coldly. "Their owners —"

"You *do* admit stealing them, then? And now you use stolen cattle for an excuse to put me out of my home!" Her tapping steps were more agitated as she threw words at him, "I was born in

154

this Territory! I've known men like you! Bullies, brave against women!"

"I'm not —"

"You are! You've been scheming to take my ranch and home like you've stolen your cattle!"

This, Tom knew in growing temper, was ridiculous. He remembered once passing a bird's nest, and bringing the small, enraged female swooping, twittering at him. Like this! He grinned ruefully.

Virginia Bratton's agitated steps whirled beside him. "Is it so amusing, Mr. Cantrell? You and your Texas gunmen trying to put me out of my home?"

"Please, will you get it through your head, Miss —"

"Do you think I'm helpless, Mr. Cantrell? When I grew up among better men than you will ever be!" Tom never did see her hand move. Suddenly his gun holster was light. She was backing away, cocking his big revolver.

"Wait!" Tom shouted. He saw her finger contract on the trigger and leaped instinctively aside as the crashing gun report shattered the patio quiet. Hot powder particles flicked his hand. The blast walloped his ears.

He barely heard her furious challenge as she backed away. "I've a revolver of my own! Try putting me out of my home, Mr. Cantrell!" She threw the gun skittering on the earth toward his feet. Head high, she turned and walked into the long living room. Her bedroom door slammed behind her.

Tom had thought his nerves were sound. He was shaken now, although the bullet had miraculously missed him.

Heavy steps pounded through the kitchen as Tom bent and picked up the revolver. Eagan burst into the patio, holding his own revolver. Eagan halted. Amazement showed on his red, bristle-covered face as he saw Tom Cantrell standing alone in this quiet patio, gun in hand.

Eagan gulped. "I thought —"

"Don't!" Tom said curtly.

Barnaby Polk hurried in after Eagan. The old lawyer's evident concern subsided as he looked around. He looked at Tom, and stepped over and picked a tin cup off the ground.

Tom glanced at the windlass post of the well, where he had placed his empty tin cup. It was gone. The tall old lawyer was regarding holes that a bullet had torn through the cup. "Shooting in the house at tin cups, young man?"

She had not meant to hit him! She had shot that cup off the windlass post with lethal aim, to warn him! Tom swallowed.

"The impulse," he said, "comes at times, evidently." He holstered his gun. "Eagan," he ordered, grimly, "ride up on the butte. I'll get back to the herd."

FIFTEEN

Virginia was furiously resentful the next morning as she stood beside her bed and belted on her blue robe.

Last night the friendly coyote yapping had retreated. Restless cattle had been audible not far away. Heavy steps, rattling spurs had moved through the house, passing in and out of Cantrell's bedroom. Curt voices had been heard. She had dropped off into a troubled sleep.

Doña Sarina knocked, and entered with a breakfast tray. Virginia regarded the food with a lack of appetite. Sarina looked at her and chuckled. "Yesterday, in the patio, he bit a chili that heated him!"

Virginia said in Spanish, "They are going to fight here with guns. You must go home to the Lower Plaza today."

"Aie! Always the men fight," said Doña Sarina, shrugging. "I fear only Apaches and *Tejanos!*" From the neck of her gaudy apron, Sarina drew a crude wooden cross on a length of cord. "The woman's tongue will do against men," said Sarina comfortably. "And I carry the knife little mother gave me! And the Cross!"

"A knife, Sarina?"

"Oh, *si!* When I was nine, almost a woman," said Sarina cheerfully, "little mother gave the knife, and said, 'When the woman's tongue will not stop them, speak with the little blade! They will understand. And always the Blessed Cross on the heart!' "

Virginia was smiling, when Sarina departed. She sobered again as she brushed out her hair and reflected on this undoubtedly dangerous day. Even Barnaby Polk had been troubled when he had heard the facts.

"It might be best to leave for a few days," he had suggested. But he had not insisted when Virginia had refused.

Her hair pinned up, Virginia gave a final critical look into the mirror, adjusting the collar of another crisp white blouse she was wearing with the black skirt of yesterday. From the top drawer of the lowboy, she took the brown envelope Isabel Alcorn had left, and carried it and the tray to the kitchen.

Doña Sarina looked at the uneaten food. "What man takes the chicken with the hungry bones?" Sarina scolded.

Absently, Virginia said in Spanish, "The girl from the fort left this letter for him. He will take her, bones and all, and jump to her rope."

"You carry the writing for her? What woman is so foolish for another? Let the stove read her thoughts!"

"Sarina!"

"Two women," said Sarina logically, "cannot have one man in the same house. You are here first!"

"If Tom Cantrell were the last man on earth —"

Sarina's "God forbid!" followed Virginia out into the warm morning sunshine.

Barnaby Polk was not in sight. Saddled horses stood tied to the corral poles, ready for instant riding. Armed men lounged in the yard. Tom Cantrell and Hampton had leaned their carbines against the well curbing in the yard and were talking. Cantrell saw her coming and seemed to stiffen.

He had washed, shaved, and changed into a clean blue blouse and trousers left from his cavalry days. His dark face still had a tired look as he watched her approach. Both men removed their hats.

Coolly, Virginia said, "Miss Alcorn left this copy of an Army report for you, Mr. Cantrell. It has information about the death of Steven Rogers, your former partner. I should like to hear what it says."

"If you wish," Cantrell said indifferently.

He opened the envelope and scanned the two sheets it contained. He frowned. Turning, he called, "I want all you men to hear this! You too, Eagan!"

The men in the yard, six of them, converged on the well. Cantrell tapped the papers in his hand. His voice had hardened.

"This is an Army report, turned in by the lieutenant whose patrol found Steve Rogers' body. Three unknown men had dismounted at the spot. Two had heel plates on their boots. One set of plates had a clover-leaf design cut out of the centers. The other set had an open, four-pointed star design, with the right heel plate worn or broken, leaving a three-point star mark in the dirt."

One of the Texans whistled softly. "Signing every step, wasn't he?"

"By now he may have new plates or new boots," Cantrell said.

Ashley Hampton drawled, "A man riding steady won't wear heel plates much."

"We can hope," Cantrell said. He shoved the brown envelope into his hip pocket. "Steve was killed between here and the Frio Plazas. The three men who murdered him probably go there often. That lopsided star mark may be around the Upper Plaza today!"

"Today," Ashley Hampton said, "we are occupied."

Cantrell nodded. His hand slowly rubbed his black gun holster. "I'll take every man to town at the first chance. We'll look for this three-star heel mark."

Cantrell, in his anger had forgotten her. Feeling unwanted, resented, Virginia walked to the corral thinking about Lee. Suppose Lee returned while these dangerous men were fighting for their lives? Lee would probably join any men fighting Cantrell.

Her gelding nuzzled through the corral poles. While she petted him, the red-faced man Eagan boosted the boy on one of the saddled horses and mounted another horse. They rode toward the Lizard Butte, Eagan carrying a mirror framed in wood. The boy looked small and important on the horse. He had been no trouble, sleeping with his small boy's dogged insistence in the bunkhouse.

Cantrell had told the Judge of the night when the boy, a furtive shadow, had drifted to Cantrell's trail wagon through tall, wind-stirred grass. A frightened, "Don't shoot, mister!" had halted Cantrell's finger on the hair-trigger of his carbine.

When Cantrell had seen what he had almost killed, he had been shaken. The boy, wearing only a breechclout and moccasins, carrying a knife and an old dragoon revolver with one chamber loaded, had been almost stupidly exhausted. He had come fast and far off the great forested heights to the south, running, walking, skulking, hiding, trying to find the Army fort which Apaches had mentioned in his hearing.

Twice this last week, Virginia had seen the boy gazing south toward the mountains where his mother was held captive. Virginia had known helplessly what was in his mind. But he had not shared his silent, withdrawn little life of waiting. Something in the gruff, red-faced Eagan seemed to have reached the boy. A man might understand, Virginia thought as she left the corral and walked to the front of the house. Cantrell had told her she could never think like a boy.

With irritation, Virginia realized that her thoughts always came back to Cantrell. He seemed to dominate this house and all in it. She put Cantrell out of her mind. The Judge was sitting in a chair in front of the house, in the warm sunshine, leisurely smoking a cheroot. He looked up, smiling, when Virginia joined him.

"Have you reconsidered about leaving?" the Judge inquired.

"I won't leave!"

The Judge eyed the blue smoke curling from his cheroot. "Women do not belong in some things," he said slowly.

"This is my home!"

"And Cantrell's home," the Judge reminded her. "He is a somewhat different young man than I had suspected, Ginny."

"I'm not afraid of the man!"

"The man would not harm you, Ginny. I made inquiries about him before I allowed you to buy into this ranch."

"He harmed Lee! He's waiting to fight the owners of cattle he has stolen!"

The Judge sounded regretful. "Cantrell has started something, evidently, which can end only in bloodshed. I'm afraid," said the Judge, thoughtfully, "Cantrell is more like your brother Lee than I suspected."

"Never as good as Lee!" said Virginia.

"As reckless in his way as Lee can be," said the Judge. "Cantrell has risked his ranch, his future, and probably his life, on a desperate gamble. He can't stop now." The Judge drew reflectively on his cheroot. His voice took the detached tone Virginia had heard him use on the bench, sentencing a man to death. "Cantrell will probably be killed before this is over."

"He has no right to do it to himself, or to us!"

"He has done it," said the Judge, gazing into the haze-hung distance. "And involved you, which I cannot quite forgive. I would advise, Ginny, going into town. If Mesilla court ended on schedule, Judge Andrews should reach the Frio Plazas tomorrow. Perhaps even today. We can meet him, and explain why his short visit to the ranch here should be delayed, or made another time."

"Lee might return. I want to be here when he does." Virginia put her hand on the Judge's shoulder. "You go. Sarina insists on staying if I do."

"It has not been my habit to run and leave the women," said the Judge.

SIXTEEN

Virginia felt stubbornly unreasonable as she walked into the house. She paused in front of the fireplace, remembering how the men had filled this long room with stirring song. And how Cantrell had stood briefly beside her, watching the fire in stern reverie, before he stalked to his room and closed the door.

His door was closed now, as solid and forbidding as the man himself. Restlessly Virginia walked into her room, made the bed and dusted. Still restless, she went back to the kitchen where Doña Sarina bustled and gossiped in bursts of cheerful Spanish.

Through the back door, men could be seen occasionally riding from the yard toward the herd. Other men returned and took up a watchful vigil in the yard. Dangerous, formidable men, grimly waiting! Shortly before noon Cantrell rode toward the herd.

Virginia ate a little meat and fiery chili. This waiting for gunfire to erupt made her taut. Cantrell and his grim men made her feel more unwanted and resented. Finally she went to her room and changed into a linen riding skirt and soft boots. From the lowboy she took a rolled cartridge belt and revolver and buckled the belt under her jacket. With her straw hat hanging on her shoulders by its leather ties, she went out back. She was in the corral, her rope loop on her gelding's neck, when Ashley Hampton spoke behind her.

"I will do that, ma'am," He took the rope. His suggestion was courteous: "Might not be best, ma'am, to ride out today."

"I will do as I please!"

He drawled, "North an' South, ma'am, ladies seem to be alike."

He led her horse out of the corral, expertly tied on her sidesaddle and gave her a hand up. He took his carbine that was leaning against the corral bars and swung onto one of the waiting horses.

"I will accompany you, ma'am," he said politely and firmly.

She made the best of it, riding north, away from where Cantrell had gone. North, perversely, where danger was expected. The Texan followed silently.

Alone with her thoughts, Virginia thought of Cantrell again; of the Tom Cantrell she had heard about at Fort Ross, the laughing, wenching, drinking, gambling young lieutenant. Yesterday, in the patio, that Tom Cantrell had seemed to stand beside her for a moment, tin cup in hand, grinning down at her as they talked of hollyhocks and roses, and the home they owned together.

Then abruptly he had reverted to the gaunt, smoldering man who was her hostile partner. His drive toward selfish goals brushed aside anything in his way. And he would probably be shot soon, as Barnaby Polk expected.

Low hills and ridges were ahead. The Texan drew up with her and said politely, "We'd best turn back." Their horses nibbled grass as he scanned the sun-drenched distance. "A fair land," he said quietly.

"I've thought so," Virginia said.

"Now you do not, ma'am?"

"I don't know," Virginia said after a moment. She reined back toward the ranch house.

They had not gone far when Virginia blinked and bent her face away from the flashing sun. A bright flick of light caught them. The Texan's exclamation was sharp: "Eagan's sighted something from the butte!"

Virginia recalled the mirror Eagan had carried toward the butte. Through binoculars, Eagan could see him plainly. He was signaling with the mirror.

"Horse coming off the butte," Hampton said. "Likely the boy."

A tiny ribbon of dust was lengthening down the steep north slope of the butte. One could visualize that reckless, dangerous rush of horse and small boy down the slopes.

"I'll meet him," said the Texan. "Get back to the house, ma'am."

He spurred his horse into a run. The mirror had stopped flashing. A second streamer of dust followed the first. A single rider was leaving the ranch yard and heading for the butte.

Slowly Virginia rode toward the house, watching the small boy come off the butte in a reckless rush. The Texan was riding to intercept the boy, and did for a moment. The boy went on and the Texan waited.

All of it was distant and toylike on the sweep of amber grassland ending at the yellow cliffs of the Lizard Butte. Cantrell must be the one riding fast from the house. He met the boy, and rode on toward the waiting Texan and Eagan, who was off the butte now.

The boy reached the ranch yard. A second man came fast after Cantrell. The Texan, Eagan, and Cantrell rode north toward the pinched-off ridges and low sugar-loaf hills straggling out from the butte. Virginia turned her horse to intercept the fourth man. He saw her intent and swerved to meet her. He was one of the lean Texans hung with guns; he grinned as he pulled up his blowing horse.

"Only yo' brother, ma'am, bringin' in some cattle," he said reassuringly. He touched his hat and went on.

Her horse worried the reins as Virginia sat motionless. Lee coming with armed men and cattle! And Cantrell meeting him! Virginia whirled her horse into a run after Cantrell and his men.

Beyond the first low ridge another brushy ridge lifted. Virginia whipped her gelding in a reckless, weaving run through the shin oak and cedar. Branches clawed at her. She had missed the tracks of Cantrell and his men. The low ridges and hills were confusing. She crossed two more ridges before she heard the distant, muted bawling of steers, and found the twisting, grassy draw which Lee's herd was traversing.

The smell of dust still hung in the air. A quarter-mile to the left, the drags of the herd were moving away from her. When she caught up with them, Cantrell and his three men were in the midst of the herd.

Cantrell looked at her without expression. Ashley Hampton lifted a hand in surprised, disapproving courtesy. The red-faced Eagan stared grimly. She counted six men in Lee's crew. At the head of the herd, Lee was riding a powerful, beautiful horse of golden coat and white mane and tail. How like Lee to return on a new fine horse!

Lee was gazing back at Cantrell with visible anger. He called to her above the bawling, noisy advance of the herd, "Look at that! Meddling in my business soon as I get on the ranch!"

"Been lonesome without you, Lee," Virginia said, and tried to make it light and cheerful.

Lee was unshaven and trail dirty. His dusty hat rode back on his rumpled black hair. The marks of Cantrell's beating had healed. All of Lee's confidence was back, Virginia saw as her sweating gelding dropped to the trail walk at Lee's left side.

"What's Cantrell think he's doing?" Lee asked with suppressed temper.

"I don't know," Virginia said, looking back. "Here he comes."

Cantrell and his men had worked out of the herd and were riding forward at a slow trot. Lee's crew began to close forward. Lee pushed his hat farther back in a familiar, reckless gesture.

"Go to the house, Ginny," Lee said, looking back at Cantrell's approach.

"Don't start trouble," Virginia begged.

"I'm letting Cantrell stretch his rope," Lee said ominously.

The feeling of helplessness caught her again as Cantrell, by accident or design, put his horse between her and Lee, at her right. The stolid Eagan pulled up at her left. Ashley Hampton and the other Texan fell in behind them. Cantrell's tired face was stony as he spoke to her. "These your cattle, Miss Bratton?"

"They are!"

He spoke to Lee. "Did you buy from a man named Fallon?"

Lee's men were arriving behind them. One could feel the dangerous tension building. Lee's thin grin masked growing temper as he called to his men, "Cantrell want to know if Matt Fallon sold these cattle!"

They grinned back. They were different from

Cantrell's men, Virginia realized. She would have felt safe anywhere with any one of Tom Cantrell's men. But not with these men Lee had brought.

"Lee!" she begged desperately. "Ride to the house with me!"

"Keep out of this, Ginny!"

Cantrell said deliberately, "You'd better go, Miss Bratton."

"These are my cattle! I'll stay!"

She never forgot his forbidding look and scornful question, "You know all about them, then?"

"Naturally!"

"They were stolen from the Texas settlements in Comanche raids," Cantrell said coldly. "I'm taking them."

"Is this some new trick?" Virginia flared. "All our money is in these cattle! You'll not take a hoof!"

"I buried men because of cattle raiding," Cantrell said deliberately. "I lost Steve Rogers, my partner. I went broke. Now I'll hit every buyer of Comanch-traded cattle. You and your brother are no exception."

Lee was reining his spirited horse away from Cantrell. "You've run your rope, Cantrell!" he said loudly. "Now I'll start giving orders on this ranch!"

Cantrell turned his level regard on Lee. "I had you pegged right, I guess, buster," he said, and it sounded almost regretful.

Ashley Hampton's voice lifted behind them. "Only seven of them, Cantrell. Move the lady away."

Without taking his gaze off Lee, Cantrell said, "This is no place for you, Miss Bratton. Leave, please! Quick!"

"Lee!" Virginia begged. "Mr. Cantrell!" Her voice was unsteady.

A new harsh urgency leaped into Cantrell's words as he watched Lee. "Let your sister get away!"

Eagan, at her left, leaned over to catch her reins. And the high, reckless shout of one of Lee's crew knifed the sunlight: *Take 'em like Lee said, boys!*

SEVENTEEN

Virginia struck her quirt blindly at Eagan's grasping hand and jerked her reins away from him.

Behind her, Ashley Hampton's blood-curdling yell filled the narrow draw. Cantrell's horse was wheeling in a fast lunge at the horse Lee rode. Cantrell's heavy revolver was swinging forward in his hand. Gunshots crashed out behind her.

Sick fear for Lee's life sent Virginia's hand to the revolver under her linen jacket. Her frightened gelding pitched and whirled. She lost the treacherous sidesaddle support and spun off, her foot catching in the twisting stirrup as she fell. Her hands, head and shoulders struck the earth as a tumult of shots and yells filled the draw.

The stamping hoofs of spurred horses were everywhere around her as her own horse reared and dragged her. Along the ground Virginia caught a dizzying glimpse of Lee's herd in awful poise before stampeding toward her. And a hoof struck her head.

Tom Cantrell did not see Virginia as he drove his horse at Lee Bratton. He pulled his gun fast enough to have killed Lee. And Sam Butterworth's remembered jeer mocked *"Soft heart, soft head!"* as Tom shot Lee's horse into a plunging stumble.

Lee was clawing out his gun when the driving shoulder of Tom's horse smashed Lee's horse into its fall. Lee kicked free of the stirrups as he pitched off. Tom's horse careened away, snorting, and Tom heard the agonized shout of Ashley Hampton: *"The girl, Cantrell! The girl!"*

When Tom looked, her frightened gelding was wheeling toward him, nostrils flaring. Her limp figure was dragging from the stirrup. *"Ah, no!"* broke from him. A wild impulse to shoot the horse died instantly — the frightened brute might fall on her. Tom spun his own horse around into another tremendous lunge.

Tom left the saddle in a dive at the gelding's head. A hand got the bridle. Both hands clamped on the bit shanks as his feet slammed to earth. He'd never savaged a horse as he did now. He broke the gelding's panic into quivering, agonized quiet with iron hands. With the reins, he iron-handed the gelding's head up and back and worked carefully toward the stirrup.

With one hand, Tom frantically freed her small foot. He shouldered the gelding away, hurled the reins away, and caught her off the ground. And only when he straightened up did he see the rolling mass of flesh, horns and sharp hoofs driving at them as the herd stampeded.

He glimpsed Lee's prone horse and at least

173

one sprawled man in the path of the stampede, and he ran for the ridge slope with his limp burden, hardly conscious of the continuing gunshots, yells, and increased number of riders in sight. He did glimpse George Sell, gun in hand on a plunging horse, and realized that others of his crew must have arrived. Shaken, gasping, Tom ran with his burden for the side of the draw and stumbled up toward the first brush.

The pounding tide of the stampede passed his very heels, it seemed. A horse screamed; a man's stricken cry lifted faintly, and the thundering stampede blotted it out.

Virginia had lost her hat. Her black hair had come unpinned. Dirt soiled her small, pallid face. Blood was oozing from a gash at her hairline when Tom halted beside a scrub cedar. He placed her carefully on the earth and went to a knee beside her.

Gasping, he begged, "Ginny? *Ah, Ginny!*"

Her head drooped over, twisting her slim neck where the silver earring had lightly rested when she had sat smiling faintly over the roses they would some day plant in the sunny patio.

He had lost his hat. Tom pushed his hair out of his eyes and reached for her wrist, and knelt motionless at the miracle of her slow, slight pulse. He held to that reassurance, almost afraid to let go.

The rolling hammer of the stampede faded in the distance. Gunshots and yells died away, and a rider dismounted behind Tom. Ashley

Hampton stepped to the spot as Tom carefully tied his kerchief over the gash at her hairline.

"Get my horse," Tom said without looking up.

"Her brother wishes to stop here and see her," the Texan said. "Want him?"

"No. I'll take care of him later. Get my horse."

When Hampton brought the horse, Tom said, "Easy with her!" He settled in the saddle, bent down, took her from the Texan, and wheeled slowly down the slope, holding her carefully. Her head lay limply on his arm. The sun struck her small, soiled face. Tom drew the folds of the kerchief over her closed eyes and held her more closely.

He emerged slowly from the jumbled ridges, and sighted home far across the open sweep of grassland. Vaguely he was aware of his crew and prisoners keeping slow pace at a distance, and knew gratefully that Hampton was giving him this solitude. He reached often to her wrist for reassurance. The house was not far ahead when her slightest stir of life came against his body. Tom bent close to catch the flutter of a whisper, "Lee? . . . Lee?"

"Lee is safe. We'll soon be home," he said reassuringly.

"Home . . ." He could feel her relax. He held her more closely and watched Barnaby Polk urge a galloping horse toward them. The old lawyer arrived with a stricken look on his face.

"Is Ginny —"

"Alive," Tom said.

"What happened?"

"Fell off her horse."

The old lawyer glanced at the armed men escorting Lee and his crew. "There has been trouble?" Barnaby Polk said quietly.

"It's over," said Tom briefly. "I'll not discuss it now, sir."

The keen eyes studied him. Barnaby Polk looked at Ginny Bratton, dreadfully quiet in Tom's arms, her eyes covered by the kerchief. The old man's face was sad as he turned his horse toward the guarded prisoners.

The Mexican woman waited outside her kitchen door as Tom rode slowly into the yard with his burden. Ashley Hampton had gone ahead and was waiting. Hampton's arms reached up for Virginia while Barnaby Polk stood by in silence. Tom dismounted quickly and stopped the woman's distressed Spanish by ordering curtly, "Warm water! Bandages!"

Virginia protested weakly, "I can walk."

Tom took her in his arms again, and followed Barnaby Polk through the house to her bedroom. Carefully Tom put her on the bed and adjusted the pillow under her head. "You'll be fine now," he said, and managed a smile. "We'll get you to the doctor at the fort quickly."

"No."

"You need to go; you'll have to go."

Her eyes closed. "You've taken my cattle," she said weakly. "You'll not take me from my home." Tom frowned helplessly, and she said tiredly, "This is my room. Get out."

Tom looked at the old lawyer and met only a stern stare. Silently, Tom went. On his way to the kitchen he met the Mexican woman bringing towels and a pan of warm water. She looked at his scowling face and hurried by.

Ashley Hampton sprawled in a chair at the kitchen table, drinking hot coffee. He indicated a full cup waiting. Tom dropped into the chair opposite and gulped half the coffee before muttering, "Who's dead and wounded?"

"Yo' Pete Yancey was shot off his horse and finished under the stampede," Hampton said quietly. "Couple of my men were shot in the meat. They are tough. More of our men busted out of the brush and flustered young Bratton's bunch. One got away. Bratton and three of his men are left."

"Bring them into the patio."

Tom was staring into his coffee cup when the Texan silently went out. Barnaby Polk entered the kitchen. Tom had not seen the tall old man angry. He looked up into icy contempt, stern in every line and wrinkle.

"Cantrell, I misjudged you!" Barnaby Polk said in measured words. "I've known Lee Bratton's failings! Of you, I expected better! Even Ginny Bratton, apparently, is not safe around you!"

Tom said, "You are entitled to your opinion, sir."

"Lee brought his herd lawfully on land owned

by his sister," Barnaby Polk said coldly. "You precipitated trouble by demanding possession of the herd. And you did it with Ginny Bratton there, exposed to any violence."

Restraining his temper, Tom said, "Her brother brought a herd of stolen cattle. And a crew of gunmen looking for trouble."

"There need not have been trouble. There are courts of law for disputes."

"Let Lee Bratton take his case to court, then!" Tom swigged at the coffee to control the dark fury working in him. "I've taken the herd and I'll keep it!" he said, putting the cup down.

Feet shuffled through the doorway. The surly prisoners were herded through into the patio at gun point.

Barnaby Polk said, "You are not the first man to believe himself above the law. In my terms on the bench, I sentenced many such men to hang! You have aroused the country with your illegal actions. By what right, now, do you hold Lee a prisoner in his sister's house?"

Tom laid his revolver on the table. "This!" he said shortly. "Men are dead back there because of young Bratton. He brought stolen cattle. He brought gunmen to take over the ranch. Now we'll see!"

"I believe you will be shot soon, young man," Barnaby Polk said, quietly. "But if not, I promise you justice in a court of law for every illegal act!" The old man stalked from the kitchen into the patio.

Alone, Tom drank the last of the coffee. Suddenly he crushed the tin cup in his hand, hurled it across the room and walked into the patio.

Lee Bratton and his three remaining men stood sullenly against the north wall, covered by revolvers in the hands of Eagan and George Sell. Ashley Hampton stood by the log well curbing, fingering one side of his yellow mustache and impassively regarding the pale anger on Barnaby Polk's face.

Lee's demand was sullen as Tom walked to him. "Do I get to see my sister?"

"Did you buy cattle from Matthew Fallon?" Tom demanded.

"None of your business! You don't scare me, Cantrell!"

Tom smashed him on the jaw. The blow slammed Lee's head back against the hard adobe wall. He reeled off and fell, and lay motionless.

"Cantrell!" Barnaby Polk said unsteadily. "Watch yourself!"

"Throw water on him!" Tom ordered Ashley Hampton.

The Texan dropped the wooden bucket into the well. He drew it up with the windlass while Tom paced in black silence to the end of the patio and back, and watched the Texan dash the full bucket of water over Lee's head.

Lee shuddered and sat up groggily, pawing at his face. Tom reached down and jerked him upright. "Did Fallon sell you the cattle?"

"Hell with you!" Lee mumbled.

Tom struck him down with another blow. "More water on him!" Tom directed.

Oblivious of the heavy quiet, he paced blackly to the end of the patio again. He saw the Mexican woman peer from the living-room doorway and close the door quickly. He wheeled back and watched water again bring Lee to coughing consciousness. Again Tom dragged the dripping figure up.

"Was it Fallon?"

Lee spat in his face. And the sober voice of Ashley Hampton cut through the curtains of fury. "Look around, Cantrell!"

Gripping Lee's left arm, his fist poised for another smash, Tom turned his head. Ginny Bratton was in the living-room doorway, holding the arm of the Mexican woman. She was small, slender, pale, in her belted blue robe. Long, black hair cascaded over her shoulders. Her chin trembled.

"Don't!" Ginny said. "We'll leave the ranch. I'll go. He's all I h-have, Mr. Cantrell!"

"Then God help you!" said Tom, bitterly. "You have nothing in him!" He stepped away from Lee, and told Ashley Hampton, "She must see the doctor at the fort. Get the wagon ready."

"Cantrell!" Barnaby Polk said. When Tom faced the tall old man, he heard an icy promise. "There is law! You will meet it, young man!"

"Tell that to the men who are dead!" Tom said blackly. He walked out of the patio and out of the house, and got a shovel and pick. Alone he rode toward the grassy draw, and the men whom Lee Bratton's irresponsibility had killed.

EIGHTEEN

Matthew Fallon heard what had happened from Lee Bratton's man who had escaped and ridden fast to the Upper Frio Plaza, where Fallon himself had come. And in the hot sunset, Lee's three remaining men came into John Hovey's saloon with word that Lee would follow, after driving his sister and their lawyer to the fort. Standing at the back end of Hovey's crowded bar, one of the men told of the savage handling Lee had received from Cantrell. "Cantrell means to get you!" he warned.

"By tomorrow," Fallon promised, "there'll be three or four men in town here for every man Cantrell has." A barber had worked on him; he had bought a new suit and eaten well. He was coolly, arrogantly confident now.

After dark, Fallon was at a table in the back corner of the saloon when Lee entered. All the swaggering, laughing confidence had vanished from Lee. He ignored the noisy men at the bar and walked sullenly back to Fallon. Lee caught up a bottle and glass and poured a drink before he dropped into a chair.

"I'll kill him!" Lee said in a shaking voice. "If

it's the last thing I ever do!" He added bitterly, "Like he killed my horse!"

"Cantrell is too much man for you," Fallon said scornfully. "Men are coming who'll take care of Cantrell. Quite a few are already here."

"Cantrell's house is like a fort," Lee said sullenly. "Even has a well in the patio. Might get their cattle back, but Cantrell can hold them off." Lee tossed down the drink and glowered at the empty glass. "I know how to get him. He'll be in the open, easy to get. He's coming to town here with his men."

Fallon clenched his twisted hand in the coat pocket. His sarcasm was barbed. "Cantrell told you his plans, I suppose."

Lee reached for the bottle again, too lost in rage to notice the sarcasm. "My sister heard Cantrell plan it. He's coming after the three men who shot his partner."

Fallon's instant question was sharp. "Does Cantrell know who they are?"

"How do I know? He said he was coming. Ginny begged me to stay away from him." Lee downed his second drink. The look he turned on Fallon was hot and sullen. "Out in the open, right here in the plaza, is the place to get him. Shoot him down like he shot my horse!"

Fallon carefully poured a drink with his left hand, and held his voice calm. "How many men will Cantrell bring?"

"All of them, the way he talked in front of Ginny," Lee said, sullen and spiteful, "It'd be a chance to take his house too. Wouldn't be anyone there but the Mexican woman. Ginny ordered her to stay and take care of the boy."

"What boy?"

"Some kid who ran away from the Apaches," Lee said without interest.

Matthew Fallon tasted his whiskey and sat thinking. "You're sure the boy is at the ranch now?"

"I saw him. It'd be a chance to burn the house; only I want that house after Cantrell's gone." Lee dropped a clenched fist on the table. "Cut him off here in town. Take his house. Cantrell won't have a chance!"

"If Cantrell did ride into the plaza here with his men," Fallon said slowly, "a few guns could cut him down from cover before he knew what was happening." Fallon sat thinking about it, finishing the drink in small sips. "There's no doubt that Cantrell would leave the boy at the ranch," he said under his breath.

"Why should he bring the kid to town? What difference does the boy make anyway?" Lee said impatiently.

"Forget it." Fallon's own heavy face was flushing from heady satisfaction. "You'd better stay sober," Fallon advised, keeping contempt out of his voice. "I'll post men toward Cantrell's ranch to sight him if he starts to town."

Fallon left Lee there at the table, and wondered scornfully why Cantrell hadn't killed the young fool, instead of letting Lee ride away with information which would destroy Cantrell beyond all doubt now. In the next half hour, to men he could trust, Fallon gave careful orders. Then, alone, he walked through the night shadows to the feed corral on the west side of the plaza.

On the soundest horse available, he rode out of town, rating the horse carefully. This night's ride would be long, and only Matthew Fallon himself could safely penetrate the frowning mountains south of Fort Ross. Only Matthew Fallon could find Senya's band of Apaches.

At Fort Ross, after the dull boom of the sunset gun, Major Alcorn paced the edge of the empty parade in front of his adobe quarters. Lieutenant Fitzpatrick, tired, perturbed and ravenously hungry, tried to turn smartly each time the major swung about.

"Miss Bratton, fortunately, was not killed," Alcorn said evenly. "A good night's rest, the doctor says, will do much for her."

"I hope so," Fitzpatrick said under his breath. "For her sake, and for Tom Cantrell's sake."

Alcorn slapped his gilt-corded hat impatiently against a leg. More disturbed himself than he cared to admit, Alcorn held his even tone. "Tom Cantrell has run wild, and capped it by taking cattle from this girl. The reports you've dispatched suggest the country to the north is up in arms."

"Tom handled them roughly," Fitzpatrick

said dryly. "Armed men are gathering in the Upper Plaza to go against him."

"How many men?"

"I can't estimate, sir. They're coming in steadily. I have two men loafing around the Upper Plaza, listening to the talk. I could move the rest of the patrol here to the fort," Fitzpatrick suggested hopefully. "We're on the north bank of the Frio tonight, a few miles out of town."

"Remain there," Alcorn decided. "Before noon tomorrow, send me a report on the situation in town. And another report in the afternoon. If armed men move toward Tom Cantrell's ranch, let me know immediately."

"If they start for Tom's ranch, Major," Fitzpatrick said slowly, "they may kill Tom before they can be stopped."

"He was one of the best men the regiment ever had. Gone completely wild." Alcorn shook his head regretfully. "Return to your patrol. Keep me informed."

Fitzpatrick saluted and walked to his horse, denied the good meal at the bachelor's mess he had anticipated. He toyed briefly with an idea of getting warning to Tom Cantrell. But habit, training, and the thought of Alcorn's vigorous anger at such a breach of orders made Fitzpatrick reluctantly put the thought aside.

Late that night Tom Cantrell paced, blackly alone with his thoughts, outside the quiet ranch house. Finally, in his room, he slept uneasily on the hard pallet of his pole bunk. Sunlight was outside the window when he wakened and rolled on his side, eyeing the wolfskins on the dried mud floor while his thoughts ranged over the past and the future.

Yesterday Eagan and two more men had followed him, and had helped dig graves and do what had to be done. Ginny Bratton had been gone when they returned.

Now Tom knew he hadn't been ruthless enough. Matthew Fallon was the key man in all this bloodletting. Fallon should have been hunted first. When Tom dressed and stepped into the quiet living room, the small walnut organ beside Ginny Bratton's bedroom door had a forlorn, deserted look. Tom remembered that Ginny had ordered the Mexican woman to remain at the ranch with the boy. He decided to let the order stand, and saddled a horse and rode out to the herd. Lee's stampeding cattle had scattered and drifted on to mingle with the other cattle.

Lee Bratton himself remained a baffling problem. Ginny's brother was no sweepings of the frontier settlements. But the years which had shaped Ginny Bratton had put in Lee reckless irresponsibility and hotheaded temper. Tom rode back to the house, tied his horse to a corral pole, rolled a smoke, and stood pondering Ginny's brother.

Eagan leaned against the corral poles in companionable silence. Ashley Hampton came from the kitchen with coffee in his hand.

187

"Will they come at us today?" Hampton asked.

"Perhaps," Tom said. "Tomorrow at the latest." He was watching the small figure of the boy moving aimlessly between saddle shed and house, scanning the ground. "What's he doing?" Tom inquired.

"Playin' Apache," said Eagan indulgently. "Lookin' for that busted-star heel print you talked about yesterday."

"More sense than we've shown!" Tom said abruptly. He called, "Look in the patio, along the north wall, son! The men were standing there! You're the only one who's thought about their heel marks!"

"A smart kid," said Eagan proudly.

The boy heard Eagan's praise. A smile touched his mouth. He ran into the house.

"I'll look too," Tom said. Eagan and the Texan went with him.

They found the boy kneeling at the damp earth in the patio, where water had been dashed over Lee Bratton. Tracks covered tracks, but the boy was tracing a small circle in the earth with his finger. Tom bent over it and made out the partly-obliterated print of a heel plate with a star design in the center. One point of the star was not showing.

"He stood in front of me and I sent him away!" Tom said bitterly. He dropped a hand to the boy's shoulder. "Son, thanks!" The boy smiled happily.

Ashley Hampton was thoughtful. "They all walked here. Which one?"

Lee Bratton had stood here! Had Lee helped murder Steve Rogers, so his sister could buy Steve's half of the ranch while Tom Cantrell was far away in Texas?

"Whoever made this print will be at the Frio Plazas now," Tom said under his breath. "Perhaps the other two men who helped kill Steve."

"Take all the men if you go," Hampton said quietly. "Do it right, or wait."

"Every man!" Tom decided. "I want him!"

Even Sam Butterworth rode with them, hunched in his old leather shirt, his long buffalo gun cradled across his lap. They were halfway to town when Eagan brought his horse alongside Tom.

"Does the major mean to do anything about the kid's mother?" Eagan asked.

"Not at this time."

"It ain't right!" Eagan rode glumly. "I talked too much," Eagan finally said. "I tried to make the kid feel good yesterday while we was up on the butte. Told him his mother would be back before long."

"Your loose tongue, Eagan!"

"He believed me, like I was his father," Eagan muttered. "He trusts me. Now I've got to tell him Eagan is a blow-mouth!" Eagan dropped back, a troubled man.

In surprised sympathy, Tom realized that Eagan was a family man now. Eagan had found

189

something to cling to, and which reached trust-fully to him. Eagan's rather barren life had become rich with purpose, despite his worry.

Ahead of them, tall cottonwoods and China trees marked the green oasis of the Frio Plazas. To the south, a rise of dust trailed a rider gal-loping fast from the Upper Plaza toward Fort Ross. Through the binoculars Tom made out a trooper who must have overstayed his leave. Tom smiled slightly over that reminder of other days. Then, as the flat-roofed structures of the Upper Plaza took shape, Tom checked his revolver and carbine and saw the other men doing the same.

NINETEEN

They pulled the horses to a walk as they entered town. And when they rode into the wide, sunny plaza, Tom cast a sweeping look at the adobe structures on the east and south sides of the plaza, and the scoured channel of the Frio along the north side.

On his last visit, freight wagons, stamping mules, cursing teamsters had filled the center of the plaza. Lieutenant Fitzpatrick's returning patrol had been watering horses and mules down the Frio bank. Townspeople had been out in the open. Now there were only a few horses and several wagons at the hitchracks. Two indolent men watched them from the shady *portal* of the Frio Mercantile, where Ginny Bratton had gone to her knees beside her brother's beaten figure.

Tom's narrowing gaze swept past Hovey's saloon to the adobe wall of the feed corral and wagon yard on the west side of the plaza, where they were heading. "Quiet!" Tom said to Ashley Hampton, at his right. "Almost too quiet!"

The leisurely tramp of their horses reached the middle of the sun-flooded plaza. Tom was squinting at the flat roofs along the south side of the plaza. He sighted a head lifting cautiously above the low adobe roof parapet of Hovey's saloon.

"Get behind the wagon yard wall!" Tom ordered instantly. "We're in a trap!"

The peering man came upright, carbine in hand. He was Lee Bratton, yelling a warning as he jerked the carbine to his shoulder, *"Now, Cantrell!"*

"Ride for it!" Tom called, roweling his horse.

Tom caught the saddle horn and slid over, Indian-style behind the horse. The spiteful report of Lee's carbine cut through the pounding rush of their horses. Tom heard a meaty slap as the bullet struck his horse. He yanked the carbine from its scabbard, and lost the gun as his horse plunged down.

Tom landed sprawling, sliding as the horse fell away from him. A spurred horse swerved violently and barely missed trampling him. The rider and a companion pulled up.

"Keep going!" Tom called thickly. He was scrambling to his hands and knees, diving for his carbine.

Lee's yell had torn peace from the town. Guns opened up around the plaza. Bullets shrilled viciously through the bright sunshine as Tom got his carbine and started a crouching run toward the open gateway of the wagon yard.

Men were shooting from the rooftops and doorways. Two men had appeared in the gateway of the wagon yard. They dodged back into the yard as Tom's men rode at them, shooting. One of the men fell. The first riders burst through the gateway past him, and swung right and left behind the shelter of the high adobe wall.

Crouching, Tom ran over to a sprawled man whose horse had galloped on into the wagon yard. It was one of the Texans, shot in the head, beyond help. Tom ducked as lead screamed past his shoulders. Bullets kicked up spurts of dust near his running feet. He heard dimly through the racket of gunfire the challenging Rebel yell of Ashley Hampton, who was waiting in the gateway ahead.

The rangy Texan held a long-barreled revolver in each hand. He was laughing. Already several of the men were firing back over the wall. A bullet ripped across Tom's back and struck dust from the dry adobe beside the gate. Gasping from the frantic run, Tom reached the Texan and levered a shell into the carbine. His hands, he saw, were abraded, bleeding from the hard fall.

"Get yo' wind while we close the gate!" Hampton said.

Eagan helped with the gate. And as the heavy plank halves swung shut, a bullet splintered through the wood. Swearing, Eagan dropped the wooden gate bar into place.

"Save your cartridges!" Tom called.

Sheltered by the adobe wall, Tom caught his

193

breath and scanned the yard. A row of stalls roofed with boards extended along the inside of the front wall. Open feed boxes occupied the south and west walls. The north side of the yard held an office, harness and feed rooms.

The man who had been shot lay on his side, dead. He was one of Lee Bratton's men. Tom jerked up a foot and found no heel plates on the dusty boot. The plate he wanted had to be on Lee's boots then, or on one of Lee's two other gunmen.

Buckboards, spring wagons, and a buggy stood in the wide yard. Snorting, uneasy horses were tied at the feed boxes around three sides of the yard. Tom eyed them and spoke with satisfaction to Ashley Hampton: "We've got most of their horses here!"

The boom of old Sam Butterworth's buffalo gun rolled through the plaza. From the board roofing over the front feed boxes, Sam said sourly, "He won't stand on no more roofs with a gun."

"Was it Lee Bratton?" Tom called quickly.

"No such luck."

Ashley Hampton said, "How'd they know we'd be here? Didn't know it ourselves until we started. This was planned."

Tom had been wondering. He guessed, reluctantly, "Miss Bratton knew we were coming to town. Must have told her brother."

Hampton indicated the horses tied at the feed boxes. "Not that many men live in town

Fallon's friends must be here."

"And we're bottled up until dark," Tom said. "And not enough cartridges."

"Got a water well," Hampton said, looking about. "They got to get on roofs to shoot in at us." He grinned again under the yellow mustache, enjoying a thought. "We're minding their horses. They've got to stay for us to shoot at."

Tom grinned too. Revolver in one hand, carbine in the other, he walked to the office, and then searched the harness and feed rooms. They had the place to themselves.

He saw Ashley Hampton digging a hole through the front adobe wall with a long-handled shovel. George Sell was shooting from a feed room doorway at the men on the rooftops. Men on the planking above the front feed boxes were firing over the wall, ducking down, shifting positions.

Tom ran crouching to a spring wagon in the middle of the yard. Screened by the wagon bed, he could see the roof parapets of Hovey's saloon and the Frio Mercantile.

Guns around the plaza were firing in fast bursts and slower searching shots. Bullets smashed through the heavy wood gate. Twice splinters struck Tom's face as bullets ripped through the wagon wood. A horse tied at a feed box back of him reared and fell. Minutes later another horse dropped.

Heat pooled inside the adobe walls of the yard. A smell of blood and death crept through the hot air. Blood had caked, dried on the back of Tom's shirt. Presently he made another crouching run from behind the wagon and got the shovel Ashley Hampton had used.

The Texan stood sweating beside the small hole he had dug in the adobe wall. "Makes a bullseye to shoot at," he said, indicating the hole. "But a man gets a view out."

"It's the best way," Tom said. He stepped back and called to the men on the board roofing, "Come down one at a time and dig holes in the wall. You can cover the plaza better."

Tom hacked a ten-inch hole through the hard adobe above a feed box. As the shovel broke through a bullet ricocheted off the blade, driving shock up the handle.

Eagan was waiting for the shovel. "Been tryin' to spot that Fallon," Eagan said grimly. "Ain't seen him."

"Don't miss if you do!" Tom said.

He peered cautiously through the new hole. A man jumped out of the saloon doorway, bringing up his carbine. Tom's quick shot drove him stumbling back into the saloon. Another man who looked like the large, untidy Ben Poole raised up behind a roof parapet. A fast shot missed and the figure ducked down. Twice in the next hour Tom saw Lee Bratton on the roofs. Each time he held his fire, and knew he was weak.

Buck Ellis was the first man who called "Who's got ca'tridges to spare?"

"You're wasting them!" Tom called. "Take it easy!"

After that they fired less frequently. Gunfire out in the plaza continued heavy. Tom noticed some of his men glancing up dubiously at the slow progress of the sun. Night was long, dangerous hours away. And not enough cartridges!

Another slow hour went by. Tom laid his hot gun on the feed box and walked to the well in front of the office. He was gulping water thirstily from the tin bucket when he lifted his head suddenly, listening intently to a new sound in the endless, slamming gunfire.

A man never forgot the brassy bugle notes, however faint, blasting the charge. Tom put the bucket on the well curbing and shouted, "Stop shooting!" He ran to Ashley Hampton, who had turned, sweating and curious beside his loophole. "Troopers coming from the fort!" Tom said.

"Chance to get some cartridges," Hampton said.

Tom looked out the loophole. "Not cartridges and not help!" he said bitterly. "Major Alcorn is moving in troops to take a hand. And they won't be helping us."

The bugle blasts cut the hot sunlight, louder, clearer. And troopers from the fort entered the empty plaza in a column of twos at a leisurely, disdainful trot. The right file bent toward the Frio bank. The left file skirted the store fronts, guidon whipping, carbines at the ready as the long, blue lines lengthened out and out.

"Have a look," Tom said.

"I have watched too many blue uniforms comin' at me," Ashley Hampton said.

The gunfire had dwindled and died away. Only the measured strike of shod hoofs filled the plaza quiet, broken by commands running down the lines.

There were more distant sounds. Tom guessed, "Major Alcorn is drawing a line outside the town too."

Ashley Hampton said, "What does that Yank major think he'll do now?"

"Whatever it is," Tom promised grimly, "it won't be good for us."

TWENTY

The two long files of mounted troopers length-ened out along the north and south sides of the plaza as Tom watched through the loophole in the adobe wall of the wagon yard. And pride came through resentful bitterness.

In the explosive quiet after the racketing gun-fire, the measured fall of shod hoofs, the easy creak of leather were the murmuring power of Fort Ross, poised over this lawless part of New Mexico. Tom had shared the lives of those men. Now, apart from them, he watched the two long files of armed troopers enclose the plaza. The vigorous, familiar commands of Major Alcorn were audible.

"Captain French! Disarm and bring out those men in the wagon yard! Captain Weatherby! Clear the roofs and buildings!"

Ashley Hampton disgustedly hurled his car-bine out in the wagon yard. "No Yanks disarm me!" The rangy Texan stalked to the well and drank from the water bucket.

Eagan unbarred the gate. Lieutenant Fitzpatrick led a detail of troopers in on foot. His black field

199

hat cocked smartly, his revolver in his hand, Fitzpatrick eyed the dead men, dead horses and sweating, defiant prisoners. Fitzpatrick's relief was visible when he sighted Tom Cantrell.

Fitz walked over to Tom. He sounded almost envious as he said, "Did you have to do it here in town, under the Old Man's nose?"

"They jumped us, Fitz. We didn't know they were here."

"Alcorn thinks you rode in for a fight. He's in a pet, Tom; came himself to handle it."

"What does he think he'll do?"

"Hasn't said." Fitz winked. "He can't court-martial you now. Probably raise a blue fog."

Looking past Fitz's shoulder, Tom said with wry warning, "Here comes Deacon French to blow down your neck."

"Oh, oh!" Fitz muttered, turning hastily.

Captain French had ridden his horse through the gate. His critical glance swept the wagon yard. Stocky, usually dour behind his heavy cavalry mustaches, French called with an edge of sarcasm, "Mr. Fitzpatrick! The major is patiently waiting your pleasure!"

"Yes, sir!" said Fitz, reddening.

Tom called what Fitz could not, "Don't get excited, French. This won't make you a general."

French, a stickler for regulations and rectitude in junior officers, reddened. At Fort Union French had thoroughly disapproved of gay

200

young men like Fitzpatrick and Tom Cantrell. He walked his horse over to Tom now and stared with displeasure.

"I suppose, Cantrell, you're proud of this," French said, breathing heavier.

"No lectures, please," Tom said wearily. "Take it out on the lieutenants. They have to listen."

Captain French turned his horse away in hostile displeasure. Fitzpatrick looked unhappy. When the prisoners were herded to the gate, Tom moved over beside Fitzpatrick. "Fitz, get my saddlebags off my dead horse out there, will you? Hold them for me."

"Did you have to stir up French?" Fitz said acidly. Tom grinned, and Fitz had to grin too. "I'll get the saddlebags," Fitz promised.

Troopers were bringing men out of the buildings and off the roofs, and tossing weapons into a growing pile. Major Alcorn, on his horse near the dead Texan, watched silently. Presently Alcorn rode over to Fitz's prisoners. Alcorn's expression was stern.

"You would do it," he said. "I warned you."

"And I told you, Major," Tom reminded him.

Alcorn's "Yes, you told me" had a regretful sound. He rode away.

Townspeople were cautiously venturing out. Tom's attention was caught by a two-horse buggy with a dusty, fringed top which rolled slowly into the plaza. A saddled horse was tied behind, and Barnaby Polk's lank figure sat

201

beside the driver. Judge Augustus Andrews, Tom guessed, had arrived from Mesilla court term.

The buggy passed the prisoners in front of the stores and turned over to Fitzpatrick's group and stopped. Barnaby Polk stepped out.

Tom addressed the old lawyer civilly, "How is Miss Bratton, sir?"

"That, young man, is no concern of yours," said Barnaby Polk.

Major Alcorn rode over to the buggy and spoke forcefully. "Martial law is in force. Strangers are barred from the plaza for the time being."

The reply from the buggy was testy. "Where did a major of cavalry find authority to proclaim martial law?"

Frowning, Alcorn admitted, "I concede the lack of full authority."

"Or any authority, Major!"

"Major Alcorn," Barnaby Polk said, showing humor, "allow me the pleasure of presenting my old friend Judge Augustus Andrews, just arrived from Mesilla."

Alcorn had not looked under the fringed buggy top. His chagrin was visible as he regarded the plump, elderly man who stepped down now from the buggy. "Judge Andrews, sir! I had the pleasure at Fort Union last year. You were with the General."

Ashley Hampton spoke under his breath at Tom's shoulder. "In Mesilla, they called that old coot The Hanging Judge. Don't look it, does he?"

Judge Andrews was in white shirt sleeves. Dignified white burnsides framed his pinkish, smooth face. He was pleasant as Alcorn dismounted. "Waiving the matter of martial law, major, what do you propose to do now?"

Fitzpatrick had sent a trooper jumping to hold Major Alcorn's horse. "I propose to restore order," Alcorn said flatly. "This man Cantrell, sir, has inflamed all the country to the north by his illegal actions. Cattle have been stolen. Men have been killed. The young lady who purchased an interest in Cantrell's ranch almost lost her life yesterday when a herd of her cattle was forcibly taken by Cantrell and his men."

"I have talked with Barnaby Polk and Ginny Bratton, Major, while we waited outside of town for this gun battle to stop."

"I can't court-martial civilians," Alcorn said, reluctantly. "But I can and I will stop this bloodshed by locking Cantrell and his men in the guardhouse, and ordering all other men to disperse."

"You'll stop nothing that way, Major!" Tom broke in with quick temper. "You're aware that all the stock on my ranch will be taken. You must know that when we're turned out of the guardhouse — without our guns, probably — we'll be shot down within five miles of the fort! Is that your kind of a trial? Is that the way you'll decide who will die? It's murder!"

Judge Andrews turned deliberately. The smooth, pinkish features framed by the white burnsides gave him a grandfatherly look. He sounded pleasant and friendly.

"Young man, you have a point there. Any criminal in the Territory is entitled to his just court." Judge Andrews pursed his lips as he looked Tom over. "Whatever the outcome of his trial," he added pleasantly. He turned to Major Alcorn. "This, Major, seems to be an unusual situation. I believe that the public welfare presses me to hold court here, and dispose of this trouble lawfully and fairly."

Ashley Hampton muttered, "He's sniffed a hanging!"

Major Alcorn frowned. "This isn't a county seat, Judge. Facilities of the law are lacking. Not even a deputy sheriff, let alone the District Attorney."

"Major, I'm empowered to hold court in a cornfield at midnight, if I choose," Judge Andrews said. "Barnaby Polk, a learned member of the Bar, can be sworn in as Special Prosecutor. Quite sufficient for such irregular proceedings necessary to the public welfare."

Barnaby Polk glanced coldly at the prisoners. His remark to the Judge held regret. "Augustus, it would be a pleasure; but I must decline prosecution of this man Cantrell. I plead prejudice from strong personal feelings."

"You draw a fine line at times, Barnaby." Judge Andrews pursed his lips again. "No doubt some other member of the Bar can be located."

Alcorn shook his head. "This part of the Territory sees few lawyers."

"Understandable," Judge Andrews said dryly. "How about your command, Major? Do you have a man with legal training?"

"Not that I —" Alcorn paused, turned, and lifted his voice. "Captain French!" And when French joined them, breathing audibly from his haste, Alcorn said, "Captain French, didn't I hear once that you'd studied law?"

"You did, Major." Some of French's dourness fell away. He brushed at his mustache. "I was admitted to the Missouri Bar, Major," French stated with gratification. "Quite an honor, I've always felt."

"Where did you practice?" Judge Andrews asked.

French deflated slightly. "I've never had the chance to practice, sir. Always regretted it."

"But you were admitted to the Missouri Bar?"

"Yes sir!"

"Excellent!" Judge Andrews said. "Major, detach this gentleman with orders to assist the court. We'll get him into some kind of civilian clothes, swear him in as Special Prosecutor, and go to trial."

Ashley Hampton muttered resignedly, "He's got us!"

TWENTY-ONE

Troopers clattered about and banged chairs and tables in Hovey's saloon while Tom Cantrell and his men sat under guard on the bar. Next door, in the Frio Mercantile, the post surgeon was using a store counter for his work on wounded men. On the mercantile *portal* dead men lay wrapped in blankets.

Eagan glanced over his shoulder at the bar bottles and spoke glumly to a rawboned private standing guard in front of them. "Flugie, a man headed for a hangin' oughta have a drink."

Private Flugelmeir shifted his tobacco to the other cheek and said, "Sarge, this here's a court-room now. No drinkin'."

Tom worked his back muscles gingerly. The raw bullet furrow was painful. He looked up when voices spoke at the guarded front door. Barnaby Polk stood there. Ginny Bratton was entering the saloon alone. Tom pushed off the bar, tossed his hat beside Ashley Hampton, and ignored Private Flugelmeir as he went to meet her.

A small white straw hat tilted toward Ginny's

eye, masking court plaster over the injury at her hairline. She wore a plain white suit, and looked small and slender, pale and composed when they met. Her voice was steady.

"Isabel Alcorn is returning to the ranch with me, Mr. Cantrell, to get the boy. She feels it her duty to see that the authorities take charge of him now."

"Best, perhaps," Tom said. "Why doesn't Isabel come here and tell me herself?"

"She feels it would be too painful after what has happened. You have disappointed her." Ginny Bratton's blue eyes were steady. "Barnaby Polk," she said, "assures me that you will have justice."

"They'll call it that," Tom said absently. He was thinking of the dreadful slackness of her small figure in his arms yesterday.

Ginny looked at his cut, abraded hands. She drew a breath. "I'll not watch your trial. I'm going back to the ranch and make my home secure."

"You'll be happy there," Tom said. His faint grin came. "Don't forget to plant roses in the patio."

Ginny looked up, startled. She bit her lip, hesitated, and turned hastily back to the front door, where Barnaby Polk waited with a cheroot between his lips.

Tom rolled a smoke, then forgot to light it as he walked back and leaned against the bar beside Ashley Hampton. He was still lost in thought when the trial opened.

In the back of the saloon, Judge Andrews sat behind a card table. At the Judge's right, a few feet in front, Captain French sat behind another card table, tugging nervously at his mustaches as he frowned over scrawled notes. Tom sat behind a card table in front of the bar; his men perched on the bar edge behind him. Rows of chairs were filled with spectators, many of them participants in the gun battle. Armed troopers lined the walls, stood behind the bar, and were posted at front and back of the building.

Major Alcorn and Captain Weatherby sat in the front row of chairs, alert and available, as Judge Andrews used the bottom of a bottle for a gavel. In a black coat now, Judge Andrews still looked grandfatherly, but he was something else now, Tom thought, watching closely. On Judge Andrews had descended the majestic, invisible mantle of the law and a judge's great authority. His assurance dominated the room.

"This court," Judge Andrews said, "is now in session. Any disturbance will be dealt with. The defendant, Thomas Cantrell, will stand."

Tom got to his feet. The coldest pair of eyes Tom had seen in some time surveyed him from under bushy white brows. "The Court," said Judge Andrews, "understands that you waive indictment by a grand jury, and formal trial by jury, which right you have."

Tom glanced over the spectators, most of whom had been trying to kill him. "I waive indictment and a jury," Tom said dryly.

"Captain French will stand."

French got to his feet, almost a stranger in the baggy black suit borrowed from the Frio Mercantile next door. A grim, dogged pomposity cloaked French. This, Tom decided, was French's long-suppressed ambition; this hour when he would finally dominate an actual trial.

"For the record, Captain French," Judge Andrews inquired perfunctorily, "are you a member of the Territorial Bar?"

French cleared his throat. "No, Your Honor. I am here by orders of my commanding officer."

"Are you a member of any other Bar?"

"I am a member of the Bar of Missouri, Your Honor."

"The Court considers your qualifications satisfactory. By powers invested in me, and for the public welfare, I appoint you Special Prosecutor in the case of The Territory of New Mexico vs. Thomas Cantrell, charged with unlawful possession of livestock. The Court understands you are best prepared to bring this charge to trial."

"Yes, Your Honor."

"Raise your right hand, Captain, and repeat after me . . ."

French repeated it, "I solemnly swear I will prosecute the defendant, Thomas Cantrell, without fear or favor. I will not knowingly suppress any evidence for or against him. To the best of my ability I will so prosecute this case

209

that justice may be done, alike to the Territory of New Mexico and to the defendant. So help me God!"

And French would try, with pompous, severe doggedness, Tom thought as Judge Andrews said, "Thomas Cantrell, are you ready for trial?"

"As ready as I'll ever be."

"Have you any witnesses?"

"Only my crew. The rest of my witnesses are in Texas."

"Do you have an attorney?"

"No."

"Do you wish the Court to appoint an attorney?"

"Not at this time."

"The Court reminds you of your right to object to evidence presented. Sit down. The prosecution will open."

French drank from a glass of water. He cleared his throat and glanced about the room. "Your Honor, the prosecution will prove that the defendant, Thomas Cantrell, about midday yesterday, unlawfully took and retained by force certain livestock owned by Lee Bratton." French cleared his throat again. "I place in evidence witnessed bills of sale purchased with drafts on the Santa Fe account of Mr. Barnaby Polk, administrator of the estate of Peter Bratton, father of Lee Bratton. I call Mr. Barnaby Polk as witness in the matter of the bank drafts."

Captain French stepped over and placed the papers before Judge Andrews as Barnaby Polk rose up from the front row of chairs and took the witness chair beside the Judge's table.

Judge Andrews scanned the bills of sale through steel-rimmed spectacles and directed, without looking up, "Take oath, Barnaby."

Lee Bratton, in one of the front chairs, gave Tom a hostile, satisfied stare as Barnaby Polk gave testimony about the authority given Lee to issue bank drafts against his inheritance for purchase of cattle. Then French put Lee in the witness chair. Coolly, Lee told of purchasing cattle from Matthew Fallon.

"Object!" Tom broke in. "Did Fallon own the cattle? Put Fallon under oath!"

Captain French glowered indignantly. Judge Andrews frowned. "Objection denied! The defendant will not try to direct proceedings. In the absence of conflicting testimony, evidence presented so far will be accepted by the Court."

French stroked his heavy mustaches in satisfaction. His questions drew from Lee an injured account of how Tom Cantrell, backed by armed men, had forcibly taken his herd. It sounded convincing. In growing complacency, French said, "I call Joe Sloan as corroborating witness."

Sloan had been in the patio yesterday with Lee. Tom had ignored him to deal with Lee. Now, closely, Tom watched the slouching, hard-faced man take the witness chair and tell his story. In the midst of it, Tom's mind wandered to the small, limp figure of Ginny Bratton being dragged by her horse.

When Tom looked up, he met the cold stare of the grandfatherly old man who would judge him. And the old man was a hanging judge! One could feel the knowledge triumphant in the room, Tom reflected, looking about. What their guns had failed to do, Judge Augustus Andrews would probably do with a lawful noose. French had caught the feeling. He was a righteous man, determined to win this one case of his life. Even if it meant hanging a man, Tom mused, watching French's confident pompousness increase.

"I could call another witness, Your Honor, to repeat the same testimony," French said. "But proof of ownership has been established. Two witnesses have sworn to the unlawful taking of the livestock. I ask Lee Bratton to stand."

Lee got to his feet. French took another drink of water and smoothed his mustaches. "There he stands," French said in solemn, approving tones. "An example of the finest virtues!"

Lee modestly dipped his head. Barnaby Polk, his veined hands folded on the shabby stovepipe hat resting on his lap, glanced up at Lee thoughtfully, made a vague, restless sound in his throat, and closed his eyes as French's voice deepened with emotion.

"The only sister of this fine young man needed help. Her faith in her brother was justified. Lee Bratton gladly used his small inheritance to buy the cattle she needed." French clenched a hand and struck the table. "What finer thing could a brother have done, Your Honor? He gave all he had unselfishly! And he was despoiled, and his sister left injured and helpless, by the violent, illegal acts of this defendant! The prosecution asks for justice, Your Honor, and believes justice will be rendered!"

French pulled a white handkerchief from his hip pocket, mopped his face, and looked around with satisfaction before he sat down.

Judge Andrews was polishing his spectacles. His glance at Tom showed no emotion. "In the Court's opinion, this makes a prima-facie case. Unless the defendant produces conclusive testimony, which will overcome testimony of the prosecution, I will be obliged to rule against the defendant. Thomas Cantrell, the Court hopes you realize the seriousness of your situation. The Court is reluctant to permit trial to proceed further without asking you again if you wished to be advised by counsel."

"There is only one other lawyer in town, and I'd want him anyway," Tom said. "I ask the Court to order Mr. Barnaby Polk to defend me."

Judge Andrews peered over his spectacles. "The question," he said, "was a matter of form. I find this most irregular!"

"I don't," Tom said calmly. "He's a lawyer, isn't he?"

"Barnaby Polk is a lifelong friend of the Bratton family," Judge Andrews said. "Barnaby represents the two children in all legal matters. He is entrusted with the guardianship of their estates, which you, Thomas Cantrell, are accused of having unlawfully damaged."

"I know all that."

The tall figure of Barnaby Polk slowly unfolded to his feet, shabby stovepipe hat in one hand. He said sternly, "Whatever this scheme, young man, I warn you now that if you are found guilty by this court, the aroused feeling of men you have wronged will undoubtedly result in your being hanged quickly to the nearest cottonwood."

Tom glanced at the rows of seated men waiting for their guns to be returned and for Alcorn's troopers to ride back to the fort.

"No doubt of that," Tom agreed. "They'll hang me and my men, or shoot us to save time."

"And yet," said Barnaby Polk, "with that knowledge, you ask me to attempt a perhaps half-hearted defense of your case, which seems lost already by the weight of accepted evidence?"

Tom looked at the tall old man a long moment. He smiled. "There's no lawyer in the Territory I'd rather have defending me, sir."

"A sense of duty to the Bar," said Barnaby Polk slowly, "forces me to assume your defense. I request the Court to grant a short recess while counsel talks with his client in one of the back card rooms."

Judge Andrews looked annoyed and resigned. "Twenty minutes, Barnaby. And during recess, the Court will allow one drink per man at the bar."

Tom picked up the dusty saddlebags which had been resting at his feet, and followed the long strides of the old man back to a card room, while chairs scraped and spectators crowded to the long plank bar.

TWENTY-TWO

Recess was over. Bottles and glasses littered the long bar when Judge Andrews rapped on his table for order. "The defense will open," Judge Andrews said. His plump figure sat more alertly as Barnaby Polk stood up beside Tom Cantrell. The old lawyer had removed his coat.

Captain French sat aggressively behind his table opposite and regarded his opponent with dour tolerance. The case, French seemed to feel, was already won. The Judge obviously believed so. This old Barnaby Polk, reluctantly defending Cantrell, would make a careless formality of it. This one law case in French's life would be successful.

Barnaby Polk hooked his thumbs under his red suspender straps and stood lost in thought while the last sounds died away in the big room. He looked awkward, and sounded uncertain, as he spoke slowly.

"This courtroom holds infuriated men, Your Honor, who allege that my client forcibly took their livestock too. Men have been wounded and killed because of it. Obviously, the angers and enmities in this room will remain unsettled until all the complaints are judged. Obviously, also, if Thomas Cantrell is guilty on one charge of illegal possession, he is guilty on all the charges. Yet, strangely, the prosecution has ignored all these other alleged wrongs and injuries."

French got hastily to his feet. "I resent the implication, Your Honor! The other injured parties did not have their bills of sale with them! It would take days to produce them! Lee Bratton had his proof!" French slapped a heavy palm on the table. "Guilt in one charge is sufficient!"

"The Court," said Judge Andrews, "was informed of these facts and agreed. And continues to agree."

"The defense," said Barnaby Polk, "will accept sworn testimoney of ownership and injury, subject to contrary proof."

Judge Andrews frowned. "Counsel for the defense will place his client in greater jeopardy if he adds further counts to the charge. The Court warns that sentence will be passed on each count."

"The defense understands, and will yield, Your Honor, while the prosecution brings all other charges against Thomas Cantrell."

"So directed," said Judge Andrews, grimly. "But the defense has been warned."

Wrinkle by wrinkle, a benign smile spread across Barnaby Polk's face. He sat down.

Captain French flushed. Then he said, "I will call every man present whose stock was taken by

Cantrell. Ben Poole, come forward and take oath. Describe what was taken from you."

"And tell where the stock was purchased," added Barnaby Polk, benevolently. "The defense will make a record of all livestock described, and requests the Court to do the same, in the interests of impartial judgment."

"This court is always impartial," Judge Andrews said testily.

Captain French, vindictive now, put the glowering Ben Poole through his testimony against Tom Cantrell. Man after man, angry and resentful, came forward and described his losses, and where his cattle and horses had been purchased. Finally French said with challenging satisfaction, "The prosecution again rests."

Judge Andrews flexed a plump hand which had been scrawling copious notes with a pencil. The Judge's comment was edged. "The Court hopes that counsel for the defense can justify all this."

"Counsel will try," said Barnaby Polk. He stood up. Sad and thoughtful, he looked at Lee Bratton. Lee's grin back was confident.

"Your Honor is aware," Barnaby Polk said in a musing tone, "that as a young man I attended school in Tennessee with the grandfather of Lee Bratton. We sparked the same young ladies. Counsel for the defense recalls that he was the better man at it."

Judge Andrews bristled slightly. "Barnaby,"

he ruled, "your wild oats have no connection with stolen livestock."

"Counsel for the defense takes note of the Court's rebuke," said Barnaby Polk, apologetically. "I was trying to make clear a great reluctance to oppose Lee Bratton and his sister in these proceedings."

"You made that plain earlier," Judge Andrews said tartly.

"An old man's memory," said Barnaby Polk, "is inclined to wander. Nevertheless, it has been a happy obligation of remembered youth to serve *in loco parentis,* almost a father, to Lee Bratton and his sister." Barnaby Polk stroked his chin. In the quiet courtroom, his voice grew reflective. "But having put a reluctant hand to the plow, counsel for the defense is obliged to open an unsavory furrow to the just eyes of this honorable court."

Judge Andrews sat straighter. His plump figure seemed to brace inwardly, and warily. "Plow, Barnaby!" he directed.

"This court," said Barnaby Polk calmly, "and all men present are aware that issues greater than the theft of livestock rest upon the outcome of this trial. More violence will be done if full justice is not rendered today."

"Justice," said Judge Andrews, "will be given!"

Captain French nodded with rising satisfaction. Barnaby Polk gazed reflectively at him. "In good faith," the old lawyer said, "this court has

219

accepted bills of sale issued by one Matthew Fallon, who does not seem to be present to testify. The sworn testimony of livestock purchases has repeatedly reached back to this same Matthew Fallon. But a stock brand is not proof of ownership. Merely notice that proof will be offered."

"This court, and also the defense," reminded Judge Andrews testily, "have accepted the bills of sale and the sworn testimony."

"Subject, Your Honor, to contrary evidence," said Barnaby Polk calmly.

Slowly the old lawyer reached a veined hand into the depths of his upended stovepipe hat and brought out a sheaf of papers. He lifted a thumb to his mouth and moistened it. In silence, as a man might deal a poker hand out on the table, he dealt the papers, one at a time.

Judge Andrews stirred restlessly. He seemed fascinated. Finally he cleared his throat and spoke an acid warning: "In appreciation of counsel's undoubted talents, the Court warns that only four aces had better appear in this deck!"

"Counsel notes the Court's long memory," said Barnaby Polk benignly, "and submits respectfully that no drawing to wild flushes will occur."

Judge Andrews flushed at some stab of memory. He watched warily as Barnaby Polk again reached into the depths of the hat and brought out two leather-bound tally books and a brown envelope. The old lawyer laid them on the table.

Captain French was watching with increasing uneasiness. Now he stared like a man partly hypnotized as Barnaby Polk slowly selected several papers from the table and fanned them out in lean fingers like a prized poker hand.

"Your Honor," said Barnaby Polk, "from the sworn testimony of Ben Poole, I am now selecting five three-year-old steers branded JV on the right shoulders, and purchased from Matthew Fallon. These five steers are now allegedly in the illegal possession of Thomas Cantrell."

"The Court," said Judge Andrews cautiously, "has made note of those steers."

"Next," said Barnaby Polk, "I offer this notarized affidavit, executed at Five Springs, Texas, by one Will Seabright. The gentleman attests that on or about the tenth day of August, last year, Comanches raided his ranch. Some sixty two-year-old steers, branded JV on the right shoulder, were run off by the Comanches. Will Seabright further attests that his was a new ranch. He had never sold or given away livestock branded JV on the right shoulder."

"Never?" said Judge Andrews, sharply.

"Never," said Barnaby Polk. "Next, Your Honor, I submit this notarized power of attorney, which authorizes Thomas Cantrell to recover for Will Seabright all livestock branded JV on the right shoulder, wherever found. In sworn testimony, the prosecution has admitted that Cantrell came upon these steers, now three-year-olds, on the open range. Counsel for the defense submits that Thomas Cantrell could not unlawfully have taken what had never passed from the legal ownership of Will Seabright. This Matthew Fallon sold what he did not own. And on this table before me," said Barnaby Polk blandly, "are other affidavits and powers of attorney covering all the rest of the livestock which allegedly was illegally taken by Thomas Cantrell."

Judge Andrews drew a long breath. "Barnaby," he directed, "bring me that mess of papers!" Judge Andrews' chagrined mutter was barely audible. "I might have expected aces all over the place!"

Barnaby Polk carried the papers and the brown envelope to the Judge's table. He remained standing by the witness chair, looking directly at Major Alcorn, in the front row of spectators.

"It is common knowledge," said Barnaby Polk, evenly, "that men of New Mexico have traded profitably with the Comanches and other Plains tribes for generations. But the times are changing. Men like Thomas Cantrell are settling in the remote parts of the Territory. They mean to develop the wild land and build for the future. They are entitled to protection, not harassment by the law or by the military."

Major Alcorn's mouth was a tight line as Barnaby Polk continued, "The defense in this trial has smoked out, and put into sworn testimony, the illegal transactions of the man named Matthew Fallon, who is not present in the courtroom. The defense will now cross-examine Lee Bratton."

Lee's triumphant confidence had gone. He was slightly sullen as he took the witness chair. For a long moment the tall old lawyer looked down at him. Then something chill and rather terrible entered the old lawyer's question.

"Young man, what kind of heel plates do you wear on your right boot?"

TWENTY-THREE

Captain French lunged to his feet, protesting, "Objection, Your Honor! The question is not relevant!"

Judge Andrews, intent on the papers, and still chagrined, did not look up. "Objection denied," he ruled absently.

Tom Cantrell's thoughts had gone to the callous murder of Steve Rogers. That fiercely demanding question by Barnaby Polk could hang Lee Bratton. Could break the heart of Ginny Bratton. And could, Tom suspected, bring enduring sadness to the tall old man who stood waiting, while Lee's sullen stare dropped to his boots.

Lee's answer was hostile as he lifted his right foot to his knee. "Take a look," Lee said. "I never wear heel plates."

Barnaby Polk closed his eyes a moment. No expression touched his face. "Excused," he said evenly. "The next witness I will call is Red Kane."

This was the second gunman who had been in the patio with Lee. Red Kane had not testified.

In a surly tone he took the oath while Captain French pulled nervously at his mustaches. Not knowing what was happening, French was flustered.

"What heel plates do you wear?" Barnaby Polk asked the witness.

Red Kane lifted his right boot. "How do I know? They was tacked on last month in Las Vegas!"

Barnaby Polk looked. "Quarter-moon in the center of the plates. Witness excused." Calmly now, Barnaby Polk said, "Joe Sloan, take the chair. And counsel for the defense asks the Court to read the contents of the brown envelope."

Slouching, belligerent, Joe Sloan sat in the witness chair. His statement was rough. "Save your wind, old man! Here's my boot!" He brought the right boot to his knee.

Barnaby Polk said, "A worn heel plate which has a four-pointed star cut out of the center. One side of the plate is broken away, leaving a three-pointed star."

"Make you feel any better, old man?" Joe Sloan asked as he dropped the foot heavily to the floor.

"The witness will remain seated," said Barnaby Polk.

Judge Andrews had been intently reading the sheets he had taken from the brown envelope. His smooth face was flushed as he looked up.

"Barnaby," said Judge Andrews, coldly, "in my courtroom, under my nose, you diverted my attention! After doing so, you dealt off the bottom of the deck, and introduced evidence in another matter. You dared do this, Barnaby, to the dignity of the Court!"

"Counsel for the defense was examining the credibility of witnesses," said Barnaby Polk, meekly. "Only justice in the trial of Thomas Cantrell is expected. Other acts of Court are outside the province of this bewildered and respectful counsel for the defense."

"Barnaby —" Judge Andrews shook his head and removed his spectacles. He cleared his throat, cast an accusing look at Barnaby Polk, and said, "The Court will rule in the case of The Territory of New Mexico vs. Thomas Cantrell."

Spectators bent forward intently. The room was completely silent.

"After impartial consideration of all testimony and evidence," said Judge Andrews, "the Court finds Thomas Cantrell not guilty on all counts, therefore lawfully possessed of the livestock he now holds. The men who purchased from Matthew Fallon have no recourse, save to recover from Fallon, if possible. Furthermore, this Court deems it necessary to request Major Alcorn to include the person and the possessions of Thomas Cantrell in military orders to protect all settlers. The Court will communicate the request to the general."

Arms folded across his chest, Alcorn said calmly, "That is not necessary, Your Honor."

"Very well, Major. And since this court is

using the protection of the Army, and is now issuing a bench warrant, the Court requests the Army to secure the person of Joe Sloan, for action of the grand jury in the matter of the murder of Steven Rogers."

Joe Sloan sat motionless in the witness chair while the meaning entered his mind. Then his lunge out of the chair met the grabbing arms of Barnaby Polk. Sloan's furious fist struck the old lawyer's middle. Barnaby Polk grunted painfully and clung. Tom knocked his table aside as he dived to assist him.

He caught Sloan as the man broke away. Armed troopers rushed to them and took Sloan. Judge Andrews hammered his bottle on the table. The flurry of excitement died.

"Court," said Judge Andrews, "is adjourned!"

Tom called out, "I'll speak now!" He looked over the room. "You've heard it's legal. You know now you've been jobbed. You'll never be safe again trading with Matthew Fallon, or men like him. I'm going to comb your ranges for stolen livestock. I'm going to break the thieves among you and help the honest men. Think it over, because my ranch is here to stay." Tom turned his back to them.

Barnaby Polk had dropped into the witness chair. He was rubbing his middle as he glanced up at Judge Andrews, who had hurried to his side. "We grow old," said Barnaby Polk. "Old and helpless, Augustus."

"I wouldn't have missed it, Barnaby," said

Judge Andrews. "You grunted like a boar hog when he hit you." The two old men were smiling at each other. "Barnaby," said Judge Andrews, "get me out to your girl's ranch, and put a hot toddy in my hand."

All of them traveled together back to the ranch, in the late afternoon. Major Alcorn had ordered Lieutenant Fitzpatrick and troopers to escort Judge Andrews to the ranch, and remain there during the Judge's visit. Barnaby Polk had told Tom, "I want Lee Bratton at the ranch while I'm there. He'll behave."

Tom rode the old lawyer's horse. Plans for the future pushed through his mind. Dubiously he eyed Lee Bratton, who was riding apart, lost in sullen moodiness, unrepentant. The mass of the Lizard Butte was ahead when Barnaby Polk caught Tom's eye from the buggy seat and beckoned.

When Tom came alongside the buggy, the old lawyer spoke thoughtfully to him. "I'm aware now how you saved Ginny Bratton's life, and how the trouble really started. I don't believe Ginny knows the real facts."

"She'll not be interested."

"Ginny is a fair-minded young lady," said Barnaby Polk. "It should be possible to exist on the ranch with her, on some sort of businesslike basis."

"Possible," Tom agreed, dubiously. "You might suggest it to her."

"I will do so."

They crossed the immense draw where the cattle were scattered out for miles. Tom was riding beside Ashley Hampton. "Isabel Alcorn's buggy is still here," Tom commented as they neared the house. "Too late for her to start back to the fort today."

"Two young ladies and some organ music would make a party to celebrate."

Tom chuckled, and lapsed into thought again. But when they rode into the wide yard behind the house, he dismounted and looked around alertly.

"Where are Isabel's horses?" Tom said, eyeing the empty corral. Then, sharply, "Something wrong here!"

A movement on the ground beyond Isabel's buggy drew Tom's attention. He ran around the back of the buggy and found Sarina, the Mexican woman, on the earth. Her wrists and ankles were tied. A towel was bound around her face.

Ashley Hampton's shout was bringing troopers and the crew galloping into the yard. Tom knelt beside the woman, barely noticing a keen-bladed little stiletto thrust into the earth.

Her hand held a crude wooden cross, which had evidently hung about her neck, inside the bright, gaudy apron. The broken cord dangled as her rigid fingers clutched the cross. Her black eyes, which had smiled so often, were haunted, frozen in an agonized stare as Tom bent over her.

Men were running to the spot. Lee Bratton,

one of the first, looked down at Sarina and said thickly, "Apaches!" Lee dropped to one knee, demanding harshly, "What happened to the girls?"

Sarina's black, tear-swollen eyes looked back at Lee as Tom unfastened the towel about her face. Lee demanded again, "The girls! Where are they?"

Tom stared at what he had uncovered. His eyes went to the stiletto thrust into the earth. Tom said, "She can't answer! Apaches had their fun with her tongue!"

Lee stumbled to his feet and stared wildly around. Cords in Tom's neck went rigid as he lifted the woman in his arms and started toward the house.

Ahead of him, Lee was already running, calling "Ginny! Ginny!" He vanished into the house.

Tom could have told him that all the big house would be silent. If mercy had been granted, Ginny Bratton would be there. But Lee would not find peace if he found her!

Somewhere behind Tom, Eagan was shouting, "Hey, kid? You hidin', kid?" But there was no belief in Eagan's stricken calls.

TWENTY-FOUR

The kitchen had been looted. Flour covered the floor. Moccasins had tracked through it. And Ginny Bratton's bedroom was a shambles. Drawers had been pulled out and thrown to the floor.

Tom laid his mute, agonized burden on the bed, and looked again at the cross clutched desperately in her rigid fingers. "Fitz! Fitz!" broke from Tom. "*Ah, Fitz!* How did they know we'd be gone this one day?"

Lee Bratton was standing at the foot of the bed. Some great, haunted knowledge bloomed and grew to conviction in Lee's stare. Lee wheeled and ran from the room.

"We'll have to get her to the doctor, and get word to the fort!" Tom told Fitzpatrick. "But first I want to question Lee Bratton!"

The drumming rush of a departing horse came through the open bedroom window. Tom stepped to the window and saw Lee slashing with the rein ends and spurring away from the ranch. Heading south, back toward town.

"The fool! We need him!" Tom shouted. He

bolted from the room and ran back through the patio.

Sam Butterworth was in the kitchen. Tom panted, "Is your rifle loaded, Sam?"

"Yep."

"See if you can stop Lee Bratton!"

Sam's long buffalo gun was leaning beside the open doorway. Sam caught it up and limped outside. He gazed after the receding rider. "Want him kilt?"

"The horse, Sam! Can you stop him without hitting Bratton?"

"Can try," said Sam. "Ain't got my rest sticks." Sam's eye stopped on Eagan. "Get down on your hands an' knees, an' gimme a rest for this gun!"

"Do it, Eagan!" Tom ordered sharply. "Quick!"

Eagan got down. Sam wet a finger in his mouth and tested the wind, and sat down stiffly on the ground beside Eagan. Sam's wispy, iron-gray beard moved in little jerks as he munched tobacco and rested the buffalo gun across Eagan's back. Sam peered calmly at the receding target. Absently Sam spat past Eagan's cheek. Eagan flinched.

"Hold still!" Sam said irascibly.

Eagan bowed his bead and held rigid, muttering under his breath. Sam was cool as he peered through the sights. Slowly, he squeezed the trigger. The heavy report slammed through the taut quiet.

Tom thought he heard in ringing ears the big .50-caliber bullet, almost half an inch through and two inches long, sing its vicious shrill into the distance. Nothing seemed to happen. It was agonizing. A miss was disaster! And Lee might be killed! Then suddenly Lee's furiously galloping horse flipped into a somersault and Lee pitched clear and sprawled on the ground.

Lee staggered to his feet and stood helplessly. "Bring him back!" Tom called. "He knows something about this!"

Ashley Hampton rode fast toward Lee, leading a saddled horse. George Sell followed. Tom turned to Sam Butterworth. "You're the best tracker here, Sam! Where'd they head? How much start on us?"

Barnaby Polk came to Tom's side. Lines had deepened in his face. "Not Lee," he said sadly. "Not this."

"Let Lee say it!" Tom said. Fury filled him like a sickness.

Sam Butterworth started a limping circuit of the house. Fitzpatrick, white with anger, came out into the yard. "The woman will live," Fitz said. "I'll start word to the fort."

"Hear Lee Bratton first!" Tom said.

Lee rode back between the two men. They had his guns. Lee's head was bowed. He dismounted in silence. Dirt from the fall covered him. He looked older.

Lee swallowed hard before he could speak. "Should have shot me, instead of the horse!" Lee

233

struck a fist desperately into a palm. "I did this!"

"Why?" Tom asked. "You were all your sister had!"

"You told her she had nothing in me!" Lee said. He had to stand a moment and get control. "I wasn't running away. I was heading to find Matt Fallon and kill him."

"Why Fallon?"

Lee looked at Tom from haunted eyes. "I wanted to kill you yesterday, Cantrell. The way you ran over me, and shot my horse. That horse hadn't done anything to you."

"It was the horse or you," Tom said. "You went for your gun. I still regret the horse. He was a beauty."

"Wasn't he?" Lee said. He sounded like a man years older, turned inward to conscience and grief over his sister. "It was me, last night in town. I told Fallon the way to get you was when you came to town, looking for the men who'd killed Steve Rogers. Ginny had told me you meant to go."

"Did you tell Fallon about the heel plates?"

"Ginny hadn't mentioned heel plates. She wanted me to keep away from you. Matt Fallon kept asking if the boy and the Mexican woman would be alone here at the ranch if you rode to town. It didn't mean anything. Fallon didn't speak of Apaches. All I wanted was you, Cantrell, if you rode to town."

"And all I wanted," said Tom, "when I left the ranch unguarded, was the man wearing that heel plate. Both of us played fools for a smarter man." Lee's haunted look was grateful for any understanding at all. "Fallon," Tom said, "wasn't in town today. Do you know where he is?"

"The man at the feed corral said that Fallon picked the best horse they had last night and rode away," Lee said. "I can guess where he went. He deals with the Apaches too."

"We met him on the trail, coming from the Apaches," Tom remembered. "Fallon admitted getting his horse from them. He knew about the boy then, evidently. And last night he found out from you where the boy was." Tom drew a breath. "We'll need fresh horses," he said to the men. "Then we'll find Fallon!"

Fitzpatrick protested, "Tom, the girls come first!"

"We'll lose the trail at dark," Tom reminded. "Tomorrow we'll never catch up. Fallon found these Apaches last night, evidently. He can take us to them tonight. Get word to Alcorn, Fitz. Tell him to meet us at the Black Butte with help. We'll plan from there."

Lee's question was humble: "Can I have my guns and go with you?"

"If you'll take orders like a responsible man."

"I will," Lee promised. He walked over to the horse he had ridden back, and leaned against the saddle, his head on his arm.

Barnaby Polk looked at him. "His grandfather and his father were good men," the old lawyer said to Tom. "There should be hope for him."

"We'll see," Tom said. He turned to the waiting men. "We'll spread out and comb the country on our way to the Black Butte. Fallon should be somewhere near town. Major Alcorn can have the town and the fort searched for him. We have to get hold of Fallon before dark!"

Matthew Fallon had turned aside at the Black Butte in the blazing midday and ridden leisurely through the foothills to Fort Ross. He needed a shave and wanted to make a check on military patrols.

This visit to the fort could also account for his absence from town. In the barbershop, at one end of the sutler's building, Fallon relaxed under a hot towel.

"Heard how the big gunfight in town went?" the barber inquired.

"Gunfight?" Fallon exclaimed under the towel.

"The Old Man himself moved out in force to stop it," the barber said cheerfully.

"I hadn't heard," Fallon mumbled. He lay excited under the hot towels. Cantrell must have ridden to town with his men. Probably Cantrell was dead. "Haircut, too," Fallon said. "Everything. If there's trouble in town, no use hurrying into it."

Later Fallon strolled about the fort, and talked with smiling assurance to Adjutant Blount. Blount knew only that Major Alcorn had moved out fast, taking most of the garrison.

It was late afternoon when Fallon rode from the fort, down the twisting little valley of the Frio, toward town. He had never felt better. With Cantrell dead, all the future was secure. Now, more than ever, the Apaches would be friendly to Matthew Fallon. He was thinking of the Apaches in scornful amusement when a detail of eight troopers and a sergeant approached on the rough road at a leisurely trot.

Fallon pulled up, smiling, to hear what had happened in town. Then he saw Joe Sloan, a prisoner of the troopers, and braced himself for some unpleasantness. "What happened in town?" Fallon inquired cautiously as the detail met him and halted.

The grinning sergeant said, "Big fight, big trial. Got one here they're holdin' for murder."

"There's no court nearer that Mesilla," Fallon said skeptically. "And the Army can't court-martial civilians. What sort of a trial?"

"Today there was court," said the sergeant. "Judge Andrews come in from Mesilla, and tried Lieutenant Cantrell for stealin' cattle. Cantrell got turned loose. The Judge told the men whose cattle Cantrell took to look to some fellow named Fallon for their money."

In his shock, Fallon realized that these troopers did not know him. Joe Sloan's baleful expression confirmed the sergeant's story. Sloan spoke from his horse, malevolently: "The men aim to get their money from Matt Fallon, soon as they catch him! And the Judge is holdin' me for the grand jury, for killin' Steve Rogers!"

"On what proof?"

"I ain't rightly sure," Sloan said. "But if I ain't helped outa this mess, I'll tell that grand jury just who paid for that killin'!"

"A man," Fallon said, "is usually helped when he needs it." The crippled hand in his coat pocket was sweaty as he waited for Joe Sloan to take the hint.

"I better be helped!"

Stunned disbelief held Fallon as the troopers went on with their prisoner. Cantrell was alive! And backed now by the law and the Army!

A little later Fallon sighted dust rising ahead, and turned his horse up the slopes. Beyond the valley crest, out of sight, he watched a column of troopers led by Major Alcorn pass on toward the fort. About half the garrison, Fallon estimated. Troopers must have been left in town.

The sun, slipping down the western sky, was still hot. Fallon felt cold as he rode on. Men at the Upper Frio Plaza were not friends now. Cantrell might be there. The law and the Army were there. When Fallon reached the Black Butte, he rode around to the towering north side and pulled up, thinking hard.

Papers and money he needed were at his ranch on the Gallinas. He could stop at the ranch, and then disappear to Santa Fe, and in comfort and safety shape his plans. Fallon reined his horse north.

The sun slid from sight in a red blaze. Indigo shadows crept over the silent earth. The click of hoofs against rocks sounded loud. Fallon had the strange, uneasy feeling of gradually being engulfed and made small in the brooding twilight.

He rode down into a gouged arroyo and out of it, and skirted the base of a rocky dike which looked like a raw backbone in the deepening shadows. And where the dike pinched off, Fallon's horse pricked up its ears and nickered.

Nerves prickled, tensed as Fallon saw a silent, motionless figure on a motionless horse, not a hundred yards away, at the end of the rock dike. He had to fight the impulse to snatch for the revolver under his coat.

Then in the fast fading light, Fallon saw that the stranger was an old man in a leather shirt, balancing a long rifle across his lap. Some harmless old drifter, evidently. Fallon pulled up.

"Who is it?" he called.

The reply was idle, "Name's Sam Butterworth. Light, Fallon, an' wait comfortable."

Memory came to Fallon in a tide of horror. He recalled that hunched figure on the seat of Cantrell's trail wagon. And the anger of the men in Largo Canyon, where this old man had helped Cantrell.

"I don't understand," was all Fallon could think of to say.

"We'll talk about it," said the motionless figure idly. "I figgered 'twas you when you

239

topped a rise couple miles back, with that right wing tucked in your coat pocket. Git down."

Fallon realized that the muzzle of the rifle covered him. Thinking desperately, he estimated the swiftly fading light. He kept the talk going. "What do you want?"

"You."

"Why?"

"I git lonesome. Light."

Fallon calculated how many jumps a spurred horse could make before the heavy buffalo gun could be brought into action, and how uncertain a racing target would be in this light. "Over there by you?"

"Don't matter."

The old man would be slow, Fallon decided. He drew a breath. "If it'll make you feel better," he said agreeably. He gathered the reins tightly in his sweating left hand and drew the twisted right hand from his coat pocket for better balance.

His shout at the horse, his savage rake of spurs launched the startled animal into a bolting run. And nothing happened, as he had calculated. Half a dozen strides — a dozen — The old man was too slow! And when Fallon heard the bellow of the big rifle, his horse was already hurtling down.

Fallon struck hard and rolled. He fought dizzily up to one knee. The loop of a rope dropped around him, jerked tight, yanked him down again.

"Rest easy," the old man's idle voice said.

" 'Twon't be long." He fired two revolver shots in signal. Two distant shots answered. The old man dismounted and limped along the taut rope. "Gonna tie your ankles an' fists. Don't git nervous. It's only Tom Cantrell comin'."

The run of a horse drummed through the gathering night to them. From the earth where Matthew Fallon lay helpless, Cantrell's figure loomed tall and gaunt against the sky as he swung off. Cantrell stepped close and looked down silently. When Cantrell spoke, his voice was quiet. "Almost lost him, didn't we, Sam?"

"He was headin' north, Tom. I ain't told him nothin'."

Cantrell looked down. "Tonight, Fallon, you're going to guide us to that Apache camp."

"I don't know what you mean," Fallon said.

"Today, while we were in town," Cantrell said. "Apaches hit my ranch. They took the boy. They also took Miss Bratton and Major Alcorn's daughter."

Fallon could have cursed in despair. Those girls should have been at the fort! He had planned carefully, and this had happened! And in all the West, there was no safety for a man who admitted a part in it!

"I don't know anything about Apaches. I haven't been near your ranch! I've been at the fort!"

"Will you guide us?"

"Cantrell, I'm a crippled man. I'm helpless here. But I can't tell you something I don't know."

Sam Butterworth chuckled. "Ain't he throwin' lies in a sweat? Tom, I seen the Utes make a big trapper talk. Half-mile away you c'd hear him screamin' it out."

Cantrell's quiet voice said, "How, Sam?"

"Tied him on an anthill, Tom. Them big ants'll eat to the bone in a few hours. They's an anthill back there a ways."

"I'm not a Ute," Cantrell said.

"You got a soft heart. An' a softer head. Y' only got tonight, Tom. An' all your life waitin' ahead to think about what a soft heart'll cost you tonight. Lemme handle him."

Something colder and more terrible than Fallon had ever heard in a man's voice came now from Cantrell's gaunt, looming figure. "I'll do my own dirty work, and live with it. Drag him over there. I'll get stake pins and a rock."

Fallon knew how it would be. They would frighten him, thinking he would talk. He closed his eyes and suffered the ignominy of being dragged by the horse and rope.

He felt the soft mound of an anthill tear open as his body was dragged on top. He locked his jaws. Near his head, Cantrell drove a stake pin into hard earth with a rock. Cantrell's hand pulled Fallon's wrists overhead. Cantrell lashed the wrists to the stake. Already the vicious, stinging bites were on Fallon's neck. Life flowed up on his face.

And suddenly Matthew Fallon realized the full fury and relentless purpose of this man Cantrell.

242

Fallon's control broke. He screamed as the crawling wave moved over his face toward his eyes. He kept on screaming.

TWENTY-FIVE

The dark mass of the Black Butte bulked ahead as their horses splashed through the shallows of the Frio. Beyond the sandy south bank a sharp challenge lifted.

"Cantrell and five men!" Tom called.

The two other men had been in the spread-out line of their search for Fallon. Signal shots had called them in. One man had given his horse to Fallon and was riding double. They rode past the mounted sentinel into deeper shadows under the butte steeps. A horse sneezed ahead. Bit chains softly chinked. The night came quietly alive with shadowy lines of horses and dismounted troopers.

A man could feel the held-in emotions of those silent, waiting men. Anger came off them in a physical wave, as it filled Tom. Isabel Alcorn belonged to the regiment.

A horse approached. Major Alcorn's vigorous voice shouted, "Cantrell?" Tom answered. Alcorn rode to them. "The man Fallon was at the fort this afternoon and left! He's not in town!"

"We have him," Tom said.

"Which one?"

"Back of me." Tom turned his horse back as Alcorn rode close to Matthew Fallon's horse.

Several sulphur matches sputtered and flared together in Alcorn's fingers. The bursting yellow flame showed the startled expression on Alcorn's drawn face.

Matthew Fallon huddled loosely on his horse. A rope around his middle ran to George Sell's hand. Fallon's heavy face was blotched with livid little bites. His crippled claw of a hand pawed aimlessly at the puffy face as the light died.

"What happened to the fellow?"

"I'm not an officer, not a gentleman," Tom said. "I tied him on an anthill. He'll help us tonight."

Alcorn's silence neither approved nor condemned. But as his walking horse came alongside Tom, Alcorn's words were introspective. "And I put off going after that boy's mother."

"A man's own home has to be hit," Tom said. "I'll need a small fire and some smooth dirt to draw a map. These nights are short. We can't delay."

Alcorn's order cut through the night; and as they rode on another hundred yards, Tom said, "Lieutenant Fitzpatrick left three men at the ranch and put his other men in our line of search for Fallon. Judge Andrews and Barnaby Polk stayed at the ranch with the Mexican woman. We decided not to move her."

"The post surgeon should be nearing your ranch now," Alcorn said. "Fitzpatrick did right. Here we are." As they dismounted, a small pile of dry twigs blazed up, gouging a red hole in the dark.

"The boy," Tom said, "drew plans of the Apache camp for Eagan yesterday morning. He thought men were going after his mother. The boy wasn't sure how to reach the camp, but Fallon knows." Tom called to Eagan, "Draw a map of that Apache camp on the ground by the fire."

"The two girls might not have been taken there," Alcorn suggested.

"Then we've lost them, Major."

They took that thought with them to the small group forming by Eagan. The fire was crackling, throwing increasing light. On his knees, with a small stick, Eagan was drawing in the sandy earth a plan of the distant Apache camp that none of them had ever seen. Only Fallon had been there.

As Eagan scored the earth with his stick, he said, "The kid says they's only about eighteen-twenty fightin' bucks in this band. A sub-chief named Senya runs it. This here X I'm markin' is Senya's wickiup. It's about halfway back from where the rocks drop off, accordin' to the kid."

"Let me have the stick," Tom said. He knelt beside Eagan. "The camp is on a large shelf, on a shoulder of the mountain, as Eagan says. The wall of a small canyon drops straight down from the north edge of the camp. East of the camp, and south of it, wooded slopes lift higher. The canyon bends around south and will block quick escape to the west." Tom looked up at the intent faces. "Surprise has to be complete, or they'll scatter into the trees. And have time to kill any captives."

Tom could feel the possibility of that torturing Alcorn, as it knifed Tom himself when he thought of it.

"They'll have guards posted, of course," Alcorn decided.

"Perhaps not," Tom said. "They'll expect pursuit and probably break camp at daybreak and scatter back into the mountains. Tonight they should feel confident they can't be tracked in the dark."

"How many hours to the camp?"

"Six hours or more from here," Tom estimated. "We go in through a canyon about fifteen miles east of here. Then up through a higher canyon to some fairly level land. At the first water, we turn upstream, keeping in the water. There's no other way. Rocks pinch in to a narrow cut. Beyond the cut is a thirty-foot waterfall with a trail around it. Then a reasonably safe horse trail works up the side of a cliff. At the top, a swing right through brush and trees will bring us down an easy slope into the camp. A dozen good men and horses could go ahead for the surprise."

"Not enough to deal with twenty good Apache

fighters," said Alcorn, flatly.

Old habits almost made Tom defer respectfully to the major's decision. But he said, "That's only half of it, Major," Tom said. "I'm taking my men into this side canyon, directly under the camp. The boy told Eagan that the Apaches climb up and down the cliff. They keep a few horses in the canyon. We'll climb to the canyon rim, and be at the edge of their camp before daybreak. When your men come in from the opposite side, we'll try to reach the prisoners fast."

Sam Butterworth said, "Mostly they'll shoot high. A man who keeps low is safer."

"He's right," Alcorn said. "All of you remember that." Then doubtfully Alcorn said, "Suppose this Matthew Fallon leads us wrong?"

"He won't, Major. George Sell will be close to him."

Alcorn stood in silence as Tom tossed the stick to the ground and stood up. A man could only guess the despairing surges of Alcorn's doubt. Isabel's life was at stake, if she was still alive. Tom knew what the man was struggling with. Tom had lived with it for hours.

"I see nothing better," Alcorn said slowly. "Captain Weatherby, pick your twelve best men and horses. Prepare to mount in ten minutes."

It was hours later, well after midnight, when Tom and his men turned their horses aside and watched the shadowy file of silent troopers pass quietly on through the faint starlight. Fitzpatrick

248

had reached the Black Butte before they left and was in the advance detail. A small wind brought a chill down off the high peaks as Tom led the way into a small canyon.

The booming howl of a mountain wolf drifted across the canyon. Tom listened and decided it was not an Apache signal. The walls of the canyon were lifting higher. Brush and trees at the top showed blackly against the serene stars. The pale sands of an almost dry stream bed wandered up the canyon at their right. A shod hoof struck rock with an audible *clink* and Tom felt his nerves tighten. In Apache territory, a man never knew.

In these brooding, pre-dawn hours, this plan Tom had insisted on was beginning to seem reckless. He was only guessing that the Apaches had returned to this camp with their prisoners. The soft creak of Ashley Hampton's saddle drew close. The Texan's quiet voice said, "We will get them."

Tom said, "Yes," grateful for the reassurance.

They were following Sam Butterworth. Reluctantly, Sam had agreed he could not climb the canyon wall with his bad leg. But Sam's instincts had been honed by forty years of this.

The boy had said the Apaches kept horses in this canyon for convenient use. Sometimes they tied horses at the foot of the cliff trail. Just beyond that point stood a dead oak tree. Farther on, the canyon bent south. Finally a horse snorted ahead of them.

Sam Butterworth dismounted. Tom did the same. Reins in one hand, carbine in the other, Tom moved to Sam's side. "Smell 'em?" Sam muttered.

Tom tried the air. "Don't seem to."

"Smoky kind of stink," Sam said. "Cold air's bringin' it down here off their camp. We'd best tie the hosses an' walk."

They moved cautiously forward on foot, skirting brush along the foot of the cliff. More horses snorted in the dark ahead and moved clumsily in hobbles. Tom presently smelled corral odor.

Sam halted as the hoot of an owl mournfully floated through the canyon. Small life rustled mysteriously in the nearby brush. Tom looked up at the sheer cliff overhead. Worse than he'd expected.

Sam gave a perfect owl hoot and listened. "Wait here," Sam muttered. He vanished without a sound. It seemed a long time before he returned. "Looks clear," Sam said. "Better'n a hour before light."

They were a battered group, Tom was thinking. Buck Ellis and Ashley Hampton's three remaining Texans were wounded. Sam's leg was bad. Tom moved over to Lee Bratton. "Going to follow orders?" Tom asked.

"I'm trying."

Tom dropped an encouraging hand on the younger man's arm. He could sense Lee's gratitude. Tom's low orders to the men were brief:

"Hampton will follow me. Eagan next. Then Lee Bratton. We're the most able-bodied."

No one argued. In single file, they followed Sam Butterworth's drifting advance to the foot of the trail, which would end, if they had luck, at the cliff rim high above. Tom led off, along a visible path threading the brush which cluttered the steep talus slope. The climb steepened. The path faded out above the brush.

Their boots made faint, grinding sounds on the rocks. When Tom paused, his deep breathing sounded harsh. Sweat lay clammy on his skin.

In daylight, the way might have been plain. This blind groping up in darkness was guesswork. Halfway up, Tom guessed wrong. A vertical sheet of rock blocked him. They had to back down. Dirt and gravel slithered from under their boots. A small rock bounced down some yards before it stopped.

Tom made another try along a small ledge, and sighed in relief when the stars silhouetted rocks above which could be climbed. The faintest gray was touching the sky. Tom looked down and could make out the Texan and Eagan. Presently the way to the rim could be seen. Tom motioned the others to wait, and went up alone, a careful step at a time.

Rock had split off the uneven cliff rim, leaving a sloping shelf some feet below. Tom crouched on the shelf and cautiously peered over the rim, through a fissure between two slabs of rock. He was looking down a slight slope, directly at the Apache camp on level ground beyond. The thatched side of the first wickiup loomed not thirty yards away, silent and unreal.

There was enough light to see other wickiups, some seven feet high, scattered along both sides of an open clearing. Trees stood behind them. Tom gestured for the men to come up. When he looked back, a pup had ambled out of a wickiup.

A tan cur at the far end of camp got up from the earth, looked toward the pup, and turned toward the nearest trees. Minutes later an Apache ducked out past a hide door flap. Eagan had edged over beside Tom, and saw the Apache. His suck of breath was audible.

The buck wore a breechclout. Red and yellow symbols were painted on his bare chest, black stripes on his face. The Apache scratched under an arm and watched an old squaw emerge from the opposite wickiup and shuffle around back.

Moments later another Apache emerged from the nearest wickiup. Long moccasin leggings were folded loosely around his muscular calves. His chest and face were painted in black and red. Lazily the Apache scratched his chest and studied the sky.

Children, squaws, other paint-daubed men began to emerge from the wickiups. Gutteral voices spoke back and forth. In the gradually increasing light Tom could sight horses tied back among the trees.

Every crouching man on the shelf had drawn his revolver. Tom moistened his lips as the nearby Apache wandered idly toward the canyon rim, still scratching himself. Back somewhere among the trees a dog began barking.

Tom wet his lips again as he peered through the narrow fissure at the Apache idly approaching them. The yawning figure moved up the slope toward the canyon rim. Tom tightened his grip on the revolver. Back in the trees, the dog's barking took on intensity. In the camp, a man called out in sharp gutturals. And the Apache reached the rim and looked down into Tom's gun muzzle.

TWENTY-SIX

The Apache's widening eyes showed complete amazement. He made no sound as a convulsive leap carried him back. He was twisting around in the air when Tom shot him. The slamming report reverberated through the gray dawn as they burst over the canyon rim.

The Texans gave high Rebel yells, more bloodcurdling than war whoops when a man remembered the ferocious Rebel charges in the late war. The other men took it up.

Only Ginny Bratton was on Tom's mind as he ran past the writhing body of the Apache. Ginny was in the rising, screeching confusion ahead, and Isabel too, if a little mercy had been given them. And now they might have short minutes to live.

A barrel-chested Apache in breechclout and paint catapulted out of a wickiup ahead, clutching an iron-tipped lance. He saw Tom running at him and hurled the lance in a lithe explosion of movement. Tom wrenched to the right; the sharp iron point of the slender lance ripped through his left jacket sleeve. He shot the man with his revolver and halted in a crouch, trying to judge which wickiup belonged to Senya, the chief. This first night, at least, the prisoners might be under Senya's control.

Women, children, and fighting men were spewing out of the wickiups. Like hornets from a kicked nest, Tom thought. The bucks clutched carbines, revolvers, shields, lances. And through the tumult, the great yells of Eagan were recognizable.

"Kid! You here, kid?" Eagan was shouting.

Tom looked back. His men had formed a loose square, advancing deliberately now, their guns smashing out shots as Apache fighters were sighted. Tom thought he heard gunshots east of the wickiups, back among the trees. Tumult around him cut off most of the sound. Then, ahead, Tom saw a squaw darting from a wickiup. She held a hunting knife.

Other figures half-hid the squaw, but the sash around her loose deerhide dress caught Tom's stare. The sash was exotic looking material, patterned in bright gold and silver threads. He had last seen it over Ginny Bratton's small shoulders! Tom knocked a frightened Apache boy aside as he ran recklessly toward the squaw.

A buck leaped around another stumbling squaw who carried a burden basket by its leather strap. A carbine muzzle swung up at Tom. Behind Tom's shoulder another carbine crashed a shot. The Apache's carbine sagged down. A

255

visible hole in his chest was bubbling red froth as he reeled backward.

A look back showed Lee Bratton levering in another shell. Over to the left, Ashley Hampton was stalking forward with a long-barreled revolver and carbine. The Texan's yellow mustache half-screened a grin of ferocity. Farther back another Texan was falling.

The squaw saw Tom running at her. She darted back into the wickiup. Tom's shoulder hit the deerhide door flap. He burst into the dim, smoky interior.

Grass pallets lay around a small depression in the center of the wickiup, where embers smoldered. Ginny Bratton and Isabel Alcorn lay on the pallets. Their arms and ankles were lashed with skin thongs.

The squaw had turned with the knife. Tom jerked the carbine up, flat side to her, as she struck with the long blade. The knife slipped over the carbine and slashed Tom's arm. His jab with the flat of the carbine struck her chest, driving her violently back. The squaw stumbled back over a saddle and household gear. Her body broke out through the thatched side, half into the open. She scrambled on out and vanished.

The girls were trying to sit up.

"Keep down!" Tom panted. He swung around and almost shot a man plunging after him into the wickiup. It was Lee Bratton. "Watch them!" Tom ordered.

He was gasping for breath, his left arm bleeding as he ducked back outside. In the pallid dawn, Tom glimpsed a mounted trooper among the trees east of camp. Bent low, revolver in hand, the trooper was riding a weaving charge at the camp.

A crouching, coppery figure retreated around the wickiup opposite, turned, and saw Tom. Red cloth circled the Apache's forehead. A red cloth streamer dangled from his left arm. Tom remembered that stocky figure looming in the binoculars the first day, sitting a dun horse on the foothill crest. There was Senya, who dealt with Matthew Fallon.

Senya's hard-breathing jump toward Tom had a sinuous flow as he whipped up a Spencer carbine.

Tom fired with his revolver. He missed. The gun clicked empty on his next try. Tom dropped it. Sam Butterworth had said, *"Keep low!"* Tom squatted clear to his heels as he brought his carbine up.

The Spencer carbine blasted muzzle vapor almost in Tom's face. And missed. Tom forced steadiness as his sights lined on the painted chest. He squeezed the trigger and saw the bullet tear through a painted black bar on the chest.

Still crouched, Tom looked past the falling Apache and saw Lieutenant Fitzpatrick gallop into the camp ahead of three troopers. Major Alcorn rode recklessly between two wickiups,

257

firing his revolver at some target. The major pulled up and looked anxiously around.

"Here!" Tom shouted. When he came upright and turned, he saw that a bullet hole had pierced the deerhide door flap at shoulder height. Sam Butterworth had been right; they shot high. "Anyone hurt in there?" Tom called.

Lee's hard, confident voice replied, "All right in here!"

"Major Alcorn has arrived!"

Apaches were fading back among the trees to the south and west, still shooting. The troopers charging into camp were making them retreat. Tom's men, their guns cocked, were looking into wickiups and finding them empty.

Eagan broke into a run. The boy had stepped out of a wickiup. "Get back, kid!" Eagan shouted. He dived into the structure after the boy.

Fitzpatrick rode his blowing horse to Tom. "They'll all be up in a few minutes," Fitz said. "How is it?"

"The girls are safe in here," Tom said. "Look after them, Fitz."

And when Fitz swung down and took over, Tom walked slowly toward the south end of camp, reloading his revolver. Blood was oozing down his left arm and over his wrist. He entered a wickiup and found a length of red calico. He carried the cloth out to a dismounted trooper and said, "Help me bandage this arm."

Afterwards, Tom moved on to the south end

of the camp and sat cross-legged on the ground, watching the full command come through the trees in a rush, and the clean-up start.

The gunfire retreated south and west, growing sporadic. After a time, sullen women and children began to drift back.

George Sell's calm, disgusted voice broke into Tom's thoughts: "What'll I do with this thing?"

George Sell sat his horse, holding the rope which ran to his prisoner. Matthew Fallon sagged on his horse. His swollen, blotched face was bent low. He swayed loosely. The claw-like right hand dangled at his side. The man was broken, not even interested in what was happening around him.

Tom stared at the sight, thinking of the grief and injury this one man had caused. "Get him out of my sight," he said. "Hold him for the law."

George Sell sounded flinty as he yanked on the rope and Fallon swayed in the saddle without protest. "I'll tie you to a tree," George said.

Tom looked away as they departed. Troopers were setting fire to the wickiups. The dried thatch blazed furiously and fell off in sparks and smoke. From where he sat on the earth, moodily smoking a cigarette, Tom could see Ginny Bratton and Isabel out in the open now. Lee was with them.

Men paused to speak to them and hurried on. After a time the rising sun found this smoke-hung mountain shelf. And presently Lee Bratton walked through the smoke haze to Tom. Lee looked ill at ease.

"I told Ginny everything," Lee said. "I'll take my medicine, whatever it is."

Tom regarded him a long moment. "You've been taking some of your medicine," Tom said.

"Ginny wants to see you," Lee said.

Tom sat undecided, then got to his feet, flipped his smoke away, and walked through the camp, carrying his carbine.

He saw the small boy standing between Eagan and a slender squaw. The boy was holding the squaw's hand and looking up at Eagan.

Sunlight fell on the squaw's brown hair. Her tanned face had a cast of sadness. But her features were not unattractive as her gaze stayed wonderingly on Eagan's red, bristle-covered face. Eagan was grinning widely as he talked to the boy and mother. Something like a smile hesitantly touched her face.

Tom smiled faintly himself over this thing which had entered Eagan's barren life. The mother would go where the boy went, Tom suspected. Eagan's life would be warm and full, and the ranch would have them all in the years ahead.

Lieutenant Fitzpatrick was talking to Isabel Hat smartly canted, his kerchief and yellow leg stripes catching the sunlight, Fitz seemed in rare form. Isabel was regarding Fitz with a familiar look, a possessive look. They would continue with the regiment, Tom knew, both of them knowing it was right.

Ginny Bratton was sitting alone, her feet over the edge of the rimrock at the canyon drop. A tightness caught Tom as he neared her. The opposite wall of the canyon was not so high as this south wall. Past Ginny's slender figure, Tom could look out to the north, where Ginny was pensively gazing. Morning mists hung about the purple masses of the distant Secundos. All the great land to the north lay brilliant in the new sunlight.

The crisp white suit Ginny had worn yesterday was now wrinkled and soiled. Her black hair had come down. The loose braid she had made fell over her left shoulder. She looked up as Tom paused beside her on the canyon rim. Her face was smudged and tired. Her hands rested listlessly on battered binoculars in her lap.

"Lee said you wanted to see me." Tom sat down at Ginny's left on the rock, his legs over the edge.

Ginny gazed into the north again. "Lee has told me everything," she said slowly.

"Everything is good now," Tom said. He eyed the binoculars in her lap. "Can you see the ranch through those glasses?"

"I tried," Ginny said. "Something seems broken inside. They were in the wickiup; stolen in some raid, I suppose." Ginny sat pensively, and then said, "I'll take your note for my half of the ranch."

"Don't fit my plans now," Tom said after a moment.

"Your plans? Who cares?"

"You own half of a good ranch. Why sell?"

"I don't want it," Ginny said, looking into the north. "The court gave you our cattle. We haven't much left. I'll not try to live fighting an angry, ruthless man, and worrying about Lee's safety. I'll take your note."

Tom shifted closer and reached for the binoculars. "Lee," he said casually, "won't be any trouble. Lee has grown up. And your Sarina will laugh again and be happy she's alive." Tom put the binoculars to his eyes. "Barnaby Polk suggested some sort of a partnership could work."

"It can't!"

"I can see the ranch," Tom said. "Try again." He had to put an arm around her shoulders to hold the binoculars to her eyes.

"I can't see a thing," Ginny said.

"It's the way you're looking." Tom had to bend close to adjust the binoculars. Smoky fragrance was in Ginny's black hair. Her small shoulder was stiff and uncompromising. "See the corral?"

"No!" Ginny said.

"I'm changing the focus. See the patio? And the roses on the new trellises? And the lady standing there?"

"Isabel," Ginny said, "might not like roses."

"Who cares? This lady likes roses." When Tom looked, Ginny's eyes were closed behind the binoculars. "She has the blackest hair," Tom said.

"Black hair?" said Ginny, faintly.

"The softest hair." Tom put his cheek against Ginny's hair, and it was soft. "Not one rose half as pretty as she is. Ah, Ginny, can't you see our house?"

Smoke drifted about them. A small smile was curving Ginny's smudged cheek, as it had in the patio that day. "Now I see it," Ginny said. Her eyes were still tightly closed as Tom tossed the binoculars into the canyon. "So nice," Ginny said. "So lovely. Tom, dear, take me home."

The employees of G.K. Hall hope you have enjoyed this Large Print book. All our Large Print titles are designed for easy reading, and all our books are made to last. Other G.K. Hall books are available at your library, through selected book stores, or directly from us.

For information about titles, please call:

(800) 257-5157

To share your comments, please write:

Publisher
G.K. Hall & Co.
P.O. Box 159
Thorndike, ME 04986